ALL THAT SHE SAW

A NOVELLA BY

ALANA TERRY

ONE

I'm not who you think I am. These are the words I rehearse to myself when I board the plane with my husband.

I'm not who you think I am. I hold little Annie's hand. She gazes up at me, her eyes wide and full of blissful adoration. She insisted on wearing glittery make-up to the wedding, and the corners of her eyes still sparkle with the tiny incandescent sprinkles.

I'm not who you think I am. The words catch in my throat. Beat through the four chambers of my heart. Pulse throughout my entire body.

People stare at us as we board the plane. I need to get used to the constant gawking. This is my life now.

Russel holds our boarding passes out like they're a crucifix that's meant to ward off the devil himself. "Here's our seats," he says, indicating two rows.

Two rows. A short courtship (Russel's word, not mine) plus a 25-minute ceremony, and I've gone from being a woman who thrived on personal freedom and independence to this. A wife. A mother. A mother of four young children, to be exact. The kind of woman who wears a head covering and skirt that reaches the floor. The kind of woman with a family that takes up two rows on an airplane.

The kind of woman people gawk at while she boards.

I'm not who you think I am.

I came so close to telling Russel everything the night before our wedding. He could see I was nervous. Thought it had more to do with the fact that his first wife's only been dead for six months, and not only am I inheriting Sarah's marriage bed but her entire way of life. The five-hundred square-foot garden. The two separate chicken coops, one for layers, one for meat birds. Up until my first dinner over at Russel's house, I had no idea there was a difference.

I'm also inheriting Sarah's kitchen utensils, her pottery wheel (not that I have a clue how to use it), and her position of first lady at Gospel Kingdom. Funny really, if you were to have known me before I met Russel, to think that I'm now married to a pastor. Especially at a place like Gospel Kingdom. Where they don't let women wear pants, and skirts must reach past the ankle. I'm not supposed to make much of myself in the sanctuary, but my new husband assures me that if I want to visit with the ladies after the sermon's over, that would probably be seen as a hospitable gesture.

I've also been informed that Sarah hosted a women's luncheon at the parsonage every other Wednesday, although the church ladies are going to be kind enough to not expect me to follow in my predecessor's steps until I've had at least a couple more weeks to settle in.

Of course, after this vacation, the church ladies are planning on throwing me a proper bridal shower. They all want to get to know the woman who stole Pastor Russel's heart after he was bereaved of his darling wife.

I'm not who you think I am.

Russel gestures with his hand, a silent

motion telling me to take the seat behind his. He and the two eldest girls will sit in front. I let go of Annie's hand, and she clambers excitedly into the window seat. Andrew, so far the only one of Russel's kids that hasn't seemed to instantaneously warm up to me, eyes me warily when I ask him if he wants the middle seat or aisle.

As it turns out, Andrew only wants the aisle seat if I'm seated in the window. We shuffle everyone around since Annie refuses to sit anywhere that's not next to me. It's musical chairs in a three-foot area. Not that I blame my stepson, mind you. How hospitable can you expect a five-year-old to be in a case like this? This little boy is already expected to call me Mom, adjust to an entirely new way of life, and his poor mother isn't yet cold in her grave. That's a metaphor, by the way. Russel had Sarah cremated. I should have mentioned her urn in my litany of odds and ends I've inherited as Russel's new wife.

Sarah's remains still sit in the greenhouse where she grew her prize-winning tomatoes. Russel assures me he'll take care of it by spring, but I haven't asked what he plans to do with them. Somehow, it doesn't seem like that's any of my business.

I love Russel, I really do. We're an unlikely pair, even more so if you were to know my entire history. Let's just say that I didn't grow up churning butter and wearing head coverings in public (or anywhere at all for that matter).

You do strange things for love.

I'm not who you think I am, but maybe, just maybe, with a lot of luck and some of those miracles Russel preaches about at church on Sunday mornings, we'll manage to be all right.

I do believe in miracles.

I'm just not sure after everything I've done that God has any left in store for me.

TWO

"How are you doing?" Russel asks, turning around in his seat to stare at me.

I give him a smile. "A little tired," I tell him. I discovered early that Russel likes it when I act a little mopey, a little weak. Heaven knows his departed wife must have been exhausted every minute of the day. I get drained just thinking about all of Sarah's barn chores and homeschool activities. Something else I should have mentioned earlier. Gospel Kingdom, where my husband preaches, acts as if any child who sets foot in a public school setting will be worshipping Satan by the time they reach their first recess.

There are some things I'm totally fine

with. If Russel refuses to get his kids their shots, that's on him, not me. He's their father, after all. I'm just the substitute. But seriously, teaching four kids I barely know everything they need for their K-12 education? Just because their dad is afraid of the big bad world corrupting his sweet, impressionable children?

In the back of my mind, I know that if we're going to make this picture-perfect family thing work, I'll have to change my mentality. I'm going to have to stop using words like *his* and *mine* and let everything morph into that nebulous gray area called *ours*.

Until then, we're definitely what would qualify as a work in progress.

I hope Russel is as patient now that we're married as he was when we were courting.

"Miss Anastasia?" Betsy sits in front of me, her blond braids streaming over her shoulders. I may not know how to milk a cow, churn butter, or lead a church ladies' luncheon, but I do a wicked French braid. Actually, six of them, seeing as how I now have three stepdaughters who want nothing more than to twin pigtail braids each and every morning.

It's the one thing I do for them that makes me feel like their mom. That makes me believe this blended family thing might just work.

I do believe in miracles. But I've learned from experience not to hold my breath.

"Miss Anastasia?" Betsy asks again, and I wonder if I'm meant to correct her or if her father will take the lead.

"Betsy," Russel says. His voice is gentle but firm. That sums up my new husband in a nutshell.

Gentle but firm.

Don't tell him so, but I think that's what made me fall in love with him to begin with. I wasn't looking for romance, I hope you understand. I can't tell him that, though, or he'll think I was using him. Manipulating him to get what I wanted. That's not how it happened.

Not really.

I love him. That part isn't a lie. But I'm not who he thinks I am.

My husband is lecturing his nine-year-old daughter — *our* nine-year-old daughter — about family, respect, and titles. She gives me an apologetic smile and starts over. "Mom?"

"Yes, Betsy?" I hope my smile doesn't look as uncomfortable as hers. I'm trying. God knows how hard I'm trying.

"Can I have my fruit salad now, or should I wait?"

Betsy is Russel's oldest, and she looks just like her father. Long face. High cheek bones. Shave off Russel's beard and cut off Betsy's braids, and they'd be indistinguishable.

Almost.

Russel looks pleased that his daughter has caught on to the new routine. That she's calling me Mom and asking me about domestic matters like the proper time to eat. I packed the snacks all by myself, I'm pleased to tell you. Woke up with Russel right at five this morning. While he went out to tend to the animals, there I was in his kitchen, cutting up fruit so his children wouldn't have to stoop so low as to purchase commercial airport food.

I check the time, my smile still glued to my face. "Let's take off," I tell Betsy, "and when the captain turns off the seatbelt light, I'll pull out the fruit. Does that sound okay?"

Russel gives a slight frown at this last part. I forgot I'm not supposed to ask the children about their own preferences and desires. I'm the mother figure after all. It's up to me to tell them when it's time to eat. But I notice the hint of a genuine smile flick across Betsy's face, and I figure I'm doing all right for now.

When Russel proposed to me, he made his high view of marriage absolutely clear. Come hell or high water, nothing but death itself would have the power to dissolve our most holy of unions.

That was all right with me. Sure, I was nervous. What bride isn't? I may be young, but I'm not an idiot. I didn't walk into this marriage blindly and assume that love itself would fuel our lifetime of matrimonial bliss. Come on. The man's been a widower for less than half a year. Don't you think I'm expecting there to be some so-called bumps in the road?

Russel also made it clear on the afternoon of his proposal that he by no means expects to stop having children. He went on to quote some Bible passage about quivers and arrows, old-fashioned stuff I didn't understand and didn't have the heart to ask about.

I'm not who he thinks I am, but I can't tell him the whole truth. Not yet. That's the problem with a courtship as fast as ours.

I hate to think that I'm using my husband. But I'm pretty sure that if you were to dig down deep, the offense runs in both directions. Would I ever advise someone to marry a widower whose wife has only been gone for six short months? Not a chance. I'm no psychologist, but I think it's pretty clear that Russel's using me too. Not in any nefarious kind of way, but in a very practical one. He needs a woman to look after the kids, to water the hens, wash the laundry, pass out bulletins at church. Pastors and farmers are similarly notorious for relying on their women to keep things running smoothly, and my husband happens to be both.

I know the road ahead of us is going to be difficult. I know there will be some shocks coming our way. Like when Russel realizes that my body's unable to give him any more arrows for his quiver, or however the metaphor works. I'm supposed to be far less initiated into the world of fertility and reproductive health than I am, so I can't tell Russel the truth.

Not yet.

I'm not who he thinks I am.

And yet I know he loves me. I see it in his eyes when he smiles approvingly at me before he turns around in his seat. Apparently, he's pleased with the way I've handled his daughter's mealtime question. I know he's looking forward to flying back to Michigan with me. To introducing me to his parents, to the infirm father and the rest of the family that was unable to make our wedding on such short notice. I know he's proud of me. I've only seen one picture of his first wife, and she looks just as tired as you'd expect a homeschooling, homesteading mom of four to be. She isn't ugly. Far from it. But you can tell farm life and the demands of being married to a pastor had drained away a decent amount of her youthful vitality.

Is this why Russel chose me? Am I simply the ten-year newer model? Is that why we're doing this, pretending to play house together? I worry about that sometimes. Worry that in ten years I'll look and act as tired and as drained as good old Sarah must have been before she reached her chapter's end.

But I can't think about ten years in the future right now.

"Mom?" Annie asks from her seat beside

me. She's the youngest of Russel's kids and has had the easiest time adjusting to my introduction into their family.

"Yes, sweetie?" I ask, feeling like I'm an understudy reciting someone else's lines.

"Can you read me a book?"

I let out my breath. Yes. That much I can do, at least. When I'm done raising Russel's kids, I really should find myself a job as an audiobook narrator for all the practice I've had.

I grab my bag. Before Russel, whenever I went traveling, I brought one small carry-on suitcase for clothes and essentials. Now, I feel like I've packed for an army just so our kids can look clean and stay entertained on this three-day excursion to meet his folks in Michigan.

The good news is that while I'm reading to Russel's kids, I can turn my mind off. Most of these books I've already memorized. Part of Russel's parenting philosophy involves a general shunning of the materialistic world. I can't say I love the idea that even books for children are lumped into the category of extemporaneous expenses. Thankfully, I bought the children books as presents when their father and I were still

dating. Since technically they were purchased with my money and not ours, Russel
hasn't complained.

Besides, the older kids have plenty of
books for their assigned reading. There's no
reason the younger two shouldn't get the
same gift simply because they're not officially
school aged yet. I'm about to remind Betsy
that she and her sister have homework to finish, but then I realize they've both already
pulled out their books.

Good girls.

Now if I can only teach them to act like
kids every so often, I'll feel like I've really
started to make some progress.

"Mom?" Annie asks, tugging at my
sleeve. It's a gesture that would make her father frown, but I don't mind. Aren't mothers
supposed to be tugged on every now and
then?

"Give me just a second," I tell her. "I've
got to find the books I packed." I'm digging
through my carry-on. So far I've found
enough food to last our family at least two
days, extra water (the only expense Russel
agreed to purchase at the airport itself), and
all the kids' toiletries, including their multivi-
tamins and an entire case of essential oils

(which I still don't know how to use properly). I even have Betsy's pajamas, which she forgot to pack into her own bag and which I tossed into mine at the very last minute while Russel was waiting in the driveway, eager to head toward the airport this morning.

"Andrew has the books in his backpack," Annie reminds me.

Right. I'd entirely forgotten. Back when we were getting ready to load the car, I made an exaggerated grunting noise when I picked up my carry-on. Really, I was just trying to get at least one of the kids to crack a smile, but Russel took me seriously and told Andrew to put some of the items in his bag to lighten my load.

Nothing like getting rescued by a five-year-old boy.

"Andrew?" I ask in as kind of a voice as I can. "May I have your backpack, please, so I can pick out some books to read to your sister?"

I'm expecting a scowl, an unkind word, an askew glance, but Andrew just shrugs then grabs his bag from beneath the seat in front of him.

Good boy, I want to tell him, although it

sounds more like something you'd say when you're training a puppy. Instead, I just smile and thank him. It's a little ridiculous the degree of relief I'm feeling that I didn't have to get into a fight with my stepson or delve into a lecture on the importance of parental respect.

Trust me, kid, I get it, I want to tell him sometimes. It's not like going from single to married with four kids is a simple transition. But I'm supposed to be more mature than he is, and I'm certainly not allowed the luxury of throwing a tantrum. Instead, I open up the book, take a breath, and start to read.

To onlookers, we're the picture-perfect family. A little stoic, perhaps. I'm sure I look strange in this head covering. People stare at me when I'm out with my family in public, but I don't care what they think.

If they knew the whole truth of who I was, what I've been through, what I've done in the name of survival, their entire opinion of who I am would change in an instant.

I'm not who they think I am. But for right now, I'm doing my best to pretend.

THREE

I'M READING Annie the same Dr. Seuss book she's heard five thousand times before. Whenever I pull it out, part of me expects Russel to tell me that he'd prefer it if our kids stuck to children's Bibles or stories with strong moral instruction. Thankfully, he hasn't taken my Seuss books away from us yet. Maybe he remembers they're the first gift I ever purchased for his kids.

Maybe my new husband has a hint of appreciation for the sentimental left in him after all.

I like to do the voices while I read, which is guaranteed to get Annie off on a giggle spree. My end goal is to hear Andrew laugh.

One of these days, I know it's going to happen. I already told you I believe in miracles, right?

I've performed these books so many times I let my mind wander off. Back to the first few weeks of my courtship with Gospel Kingdom's recently widowed pastor.

I was new to town. New to a lot of things, truth be told. I'd put on weight, partly due to stress, partly due to the fact that I was still terrified of being recognized. With this head covering, people don't stop me anymore. Don't ask me why I look so familiar.

Don't look at me with a mix of both pity and fear when they realize who I truly am.

I wasn't an obvious candidate for the secretary opening at Gospel Kingdom. I responded to an ad in the paper and showed up to my interview wearing a gray pants suit. That was strike number one.

"Is this a Mennonite church?" I asked Russel when I saw the photo in his office of his congregants posing in front of the spotless, white steeple.

He gave a little chuckle, which led me to believe that this man was always that easy to laugh. "No, not Mennonite, although you certainly wouldn't be the first to jump to that sort of conclusion."

I apologized for wearing trousers, for not having my head covering. I acted as if I had a closet full of floor-length skirts and color-coordinated hair kerchiefs to match, but Russel told me not to worry.

"It's an old-fashioned dress code," he explained, "but we're a family here, and we like our traditional ways." Somehow he managed to speak these words, to sum up the entire personality of his church in a single word — *traditional* — and yet did so without making me feel at all inferior or ashamed of my more contemporary appearance.

"Can you tell me about your spiritual journey?" Russel asked. It wouldn't have boded well for my prospects at landing a job if I were to tell him that honestly, I thought about spirituality as much as I thought about garden slugs or tennis-ball-sized hail. So I offered some sort of noncommittal response like, "Oh, well, I grew up going to church pretty regularly, then kind of fell away … Still love God, just haven't been connected to an actual congregation for a while."

Before I knew it, Russel had opened up

his Bible, set it on the table between us, and was explaining to me truths about Jesus I'd never heard before. Answering questions about the Lord that I never even realized I was wondering.

"Do you want to ask Jesus to forgive your sins? Are you ready to make him Lord of your life?" he prompted.

I told him yes, but it wasn't just to land the job. And it wasn't that strange magnetic force I felt when we were talking together. I think those things may have played a part, but there was more to it than that.

Far more to it.

I've always believed in God. Even during those two years I've never told my husband about, when it seemed like everything had been taken away from me, I had a sense that God was there. That he was with me. That he would somehow see me through the hell on earth where I was trapped.

But when Russel talked about Jesus, I realized this man knew the Lord far more deeply than I ever dreamed possible. So I told him yes, I wanted what he had. Then I prayed with him. Recited this little prayer about getting God to forgive my sins, saving me from hell. Russel looked pleased with me when I was done, and that's when I knew that if I got this job as his secretary, I'd keep on trying to find ways to make him smile at me like that.

No matter what it took.

No matter what I had to give up.

I started working at the church office the very next day. In addition to helping Russel print bulletins, schedule appointments, pay the bills, I sat at his feet (in the metaphorical sense at least), learning daily from him as he led our little office "staff" (consisting only of him and me) in morning Bible study, in closing prayers at the end of the day.

I wasn't deliberately keeping my past from him. But things moved so quickly from there. I was excited about my newfound faith, and it was impossible to distinguish my spiritual awakening with the emotional connection I felt with Russel whenever the two of us were together.

We fell in love. Before we'd even known each other a full season, he introduced me to his children, proposed courtship, then announced our engagement to the entire congregation.

And now here I am. Stepmother of four, struggling to work my way into this family that managed to get along swimmingly on their own before I came around. A grateful bride, thankful for the sense of protection and security that comes from belonging to Russel and his family and his church, even if they are a little strict by worldly standards.

I'm happy to be with Russel. I'm happy to call his children my own. Once we return from meeting his side of the family, Russel wants me to adopt the kids. I'm not one to argue. I'll never be able to bear Russel the quiver full of offspring his heart is set on. The least I can do is formalize my relationship to the four he already has.

I'm not who he thinks I am.

But maybe, with a little luck, a lot of prayer, and some very powerful miracles, things will work out all right in the end.

Maybe, just maybe, I'll look back on these past few months and realize how blessed I really am.

And if Russel finds out the truth … Well, isn't he the one who said that we're united now? That nothing but death will ever part us?

I keep waiting for the day when I'll wake up and actually feel like Anastasia Strickland, wife of Gospel Kingdom's pastor. When I can look at Russel's kids and not feel the pangs of guilt at my deception when they call me Mom.

And if that day never comes, I just have to remind myself it at least beats where I came from.

The Lord works in mysterious ways. Maybe, just maybe, he brought me to Russel and his kind, albeit quirky little church in order to offer me the stability and protection I needed so many years ago, those days I'm trying so hard to forget.

Is it possible that Russel felt like a safe option for me because of the way he and the others at his church avoid technology as much as they do? I admit, the fact that Russel wouldn't ever think to google my name or stumble across news articles from ten years ago was an added bonus when we started dating.

I'm not who my husband thinks I am. But maybe, just maybe, if I pray hard enough and try hard enough, God will help me turn into the person he wants me to be.

And then everything from the past can stay there in the past. Totally secret.

Totally forgotten.

Just the way it should be.

Just the way it needs to be.

FOUR

I'm NOT who he thinks I am, but no matter how hard I cry, how fiercely or angrily I protest, he doesn't listen to me. Doesn't believe me.

"Jennifer," he says, "you know how angry I get when you're like this."

"My name isn't Jennifer." It doesn't matter if I scream it at him, if I curse and swear, if I break down into tears and beg him to believe me.

"Come on, Jennifer," he says. "Stop pretending like you don't know your own dad and come here."

I hate him. I hate him. My loathing is the only source of willpower it takes to stay alive down here, trapped in this basement. If

I were any weaker, I know I would have died by now.

My survival depends on one thing and one thing only. The hope that one day he'll forget to bind me up the right way. That I'll find some kind of weapon in this horrid cell of his.

And then I'll kill him, screaming in his face as his breath deserts him for the very last time, "My name isn't Jennifer!"

"Mom?"

I jerk myself to attention. "What?"

It's Annie, looking at me with concern in her eyes. Even Andrew has stopped ignoring me in order to gawk a little. Have I done it again? Did I blip out?

I can't let things like this keep happening. Not when the kids are around.

"Mom?"

"What?" I ask, doing my best to shake off this fear, this pulse-quickening panic.

"You stopped reading." Annie points to the book. I don't even remember pulling this one out of Andrew's backpack. The last thing I remember was Dr. Seuss and then …

And then …

It must have been Henry. He's been dead

these past ten years, and yet he still lives on in my head.

If I had known it would turn out like this …

No. I can't focus on him. Have to keep reading to the kids. I shouldn't have picked such a familiar book. Too easy for my brain to turn off. To stop paying attention to what's going on right now.

Henry.

Almost nobody survives two full years of captivity. I'm an anomaly, a strange statistic. My story gives hope to parents whose children disappeared decades ago.

If that little Reynolds girl can come back from her ordeal, there's hope for my baby too.

What they don't know, what the news reporters and the family liaisons and the sensationalized docudramas don't tell you is that survival in cases like this can be seen as God's cruelest curse. How many times did I beg Henry to simply kill me? To get it done and over with quickly. How many times did I taunt him, trying my hardest to provoke him to enough rage that he'd finally end it all?

Except he never did. I was too important to him. Too much like his long-lost daughter.

Jennifer. The dead child I was meant to replace.

After my escape, I went through a phase where I hated her. Hated Jennifer. She would have been twice my age, but in her father's sick mind she was still the age she was when she was murdered.

Nobody back then was convicted of her death.

And yet I'm the one who paid for it.

Henry and I both paid for it.

"Mom, you read that page already." Andrew's voice is whiny, and I'm too distracted by these daydreams to feel excited about the fact that he's voluntarily called me Mom without having to be reminded. It should be good news. A great step forward in our quest for familial unity.

And yet all I can think about is that we haven't even left the runway yet. A few stray passengers are still boarding, and the kids and I have hours of travel ahead of us. Russel has the easy job. He'll fall asleep with his Bible while the two older girls read quietly in their seats. And here I am with a squirrely little preschooler who can't go two minutes without asking me a dozen questions and her five-year-old brother who wants nothing more than to make my life miserable enough that I abandon his father and leave him alone to miss his mom in uninterrupted solitude.

I feel sorry for Andrew. I really do. My parents split up shortly after I escaped Henry's basement. Dad didn't remarry until a few years ago, and even now it's strange to picture him with someone else.

I need to stop thinking about my past. Need to focus on what those books about trauma say. I survived because I'm tough. I'm a fighter. I'm a warrior. I did what I had to do to survive, and nobody has the power to victimize me ever again.

I think I believe it. I want to believe it.

But sometimes I still wonder.

I think Russel would understand if I told him the first part. If I told him that the reason I don't talk about my high school years is because half of them were spent chained in a crazy man's basement, and after that I never resumed my public education. I could tell him about how Henry dressed me up in his daughter Jennifer's clothes, fashions that hadn't been in style in nearly two decades. Nobody would understand unless they've lived through that kind of torment, and like I said before, I'm the statistical anomaly.

My husband wouldn't understand, but that doesn't mean he wouldn't care. He would listen with those kind, compassionate eyes. It's his empathy that makes him such a good pastor. He's the only reason a church as stuck in its ways and traditional as ours can still flourish and prosper. Gospel Kingdom would only work if the members absolutely love and respect their leader. Which they do.

And with good reason.

Russel would try to empathize with the trauma I've gone through. He's as patient as a saint with me already, and that's without knowing anything I've endured.

I should tell him. I would tell him. Except that would lead to other questions. Like how I got myself out of Henry's basement. How I survived when so many others like me didn't.

And then he'd realize I've lied to him about other things, too. Like how excited I am to start a family with him. He still thinks I'm going to be able to bear him a quiver full of children. How long will I be able to pretend like this before he grows suspicious?

I should never have misled my husband. I should never have agreed to marry him so quickly. It all happened so fast I can hardly remember what life was like before we met. It was as if I woke up single, and in twelve hours I was fumbling around through the world's most painfully awkward wedding night. Now there are kids calling me Mom, kids I'm responsible to clothe and feed and educate. What do I know about homeschooling? Russel's showed me the curriculum Sarah used with the older kids, but I'm serious that you need an advanced degree just to understand the teacher's manual.

It's a good thing I have God on my side now. I'm not convinced the Almighty has forgiven me for lying to my husband, but I hope that he won't take it out on the children. It is not their fault. And Russel's devoted his life to preaching to others. He does it so well too. Just look how he ended up converting me.

I've risen to greater challenges than this. Heaven knows that's true even if my husband doesn't. The way I figure, if God wants to develop my character by throwing me into a scenario where I've adopted four kids who aren't my own and agreed to homeschool them and raise them up in a tech-free, sugar-free, wordly-influence-free environment, well, it won't be the hardest thing I've ever gone through.

Not by a longshot.

I survived two years in Henry's basement.

I survived two years calling him *Daddy*, pretending to be his murdered daughter, wearing clothes that were two decades too old.

I survived the beatings, the assaults, all of it.

More than that. I escaped.

I escaped because I'm tough. I'm a fighter. I'm a warrior. I did what I had to do to survive, and nobody has the power to victimize me again.

I repeat the words to myself. If I can handle myself with a monster like Henry, I'm not going to let a somewhat uppity church and a houseful of kids who aren't sure how they feel about me ruin my chances at happiness.

When I met Russel, I was drawn to his compassion, to his conviction, to the safety and security I felt in his presence. But that's not why I married him. I married him because I love him. And if it's going to take work to make this happily-ever-after thing work, if it means sitting on this airplane for hours with his kids and doing my best to entertain them and keep them quiet and calm so their father can sleep, I can deal with that.

God knows I've fought my way out of worse.

FIVE

THERE'S some kind of delay on the runway. Could be the weather. I hear there's snow-storms all over the Midwest right now. Just perfect for flying into Detroit, right? I stop reading long enough to check the time.

Russel turns around in his seat. "Are you all right?" he asks. I'm not sure what prompted him to check up on me like this. Did he hear me stop reading and wonder what was going on? Did he sense the dark thoughts I've been having?

It's like this sometimes. I can go weeks hardly thinking about Henry at all. In fact, until I started having panic attacks a couple years ago, I thought I was over my past entirely.

Shows how naïve I was.

I smile at my husband, worried that his compassionate eyes will see straight through me. That he'll know what I'm keeping from him, the truth about what I did in order to become the survivor I am.

"I'm all right," I answer, "just tired."

That seems to be all he needs to hear. He reaches out for my hand. The gesture is surprisingly gentle. He's usually not one for public displays of affection. I'm glad to see him looking happy and content. I hope this vacation does him good. He's been under a lot of stress. I feel bad, like it's my fault. Like a good wife would anticipate her husband's needs well enough in advance to keep his life running smoothly.

Was Sarah that kind of wife? I wonder. Was she the kind who always had a home-cooked meal ready for him at exactly the same time every evening? Who tucked their children into bed after an elaborate routine that was full of love and attention and care?

Russel doesn't talk about his first wife. Doesn't tell me what it was like as Sarah was dying, how the children reacted to the news of her passing. I don't bring it up. I'm afraid that if I did, I'd see that sadness in his eyes.

A sadness that I can't take away no matter how hard I might try to fill the hole in Russel's heart.

The captain makes an announcement. We'll be on our way soon. It's about time. I'd be lying if I said I wasn't nervous about meeting Russel's family, but I also have no desire to sit here in a grounded airplane for the rest of my life. I've never flown with kids before. Wonder what will happen when Andrew needs to use the bathroom. Will he want me to take him or his father? Do I have to go in with him, or do I just wait outside the door?

Again I picture Sarah. Tired, haggered Sarah, aged beyond her years. Did she like wearing her head-coverings? Did she mind the way her long skirts always got bunched up around her ankles? Maybe she grew up that way, so she never knew any differently. I don't even know where she was from or if her mom or dad are still alive. If the kids have grandparents from that side of the family, is it now my job to make sure they stay connected?

There are so many things for me to think about, so many plans I need to make. Russel and I are basically still on our honeymoon, but after this trip to Detroit, it's the start of normal life. There are so many things I need to figure out. How to schedule our homeschool days so that we have some semblance of order. What to do with the younger kids while I'm working with the older ones on their lessons. I haven't mentioned this to Russel yet, but math was never my strong suit. Before too long, Betsy's going to have to ask somebody else for help.

I take a deep breath. Remind myself that nobody's doing any math lessons today. We're all fine. We're here, we're healthy, we're safe.

Safe …

I sense the change in the cabin before I see anything out of the ordinary. A tension. A kind of electric charge. It would be easy enough to dismiss if I weren't already on edge.

I look around, hunting for the source of my unease. Something's wrong. Something happened …

Then I see him.

SIX

THEY LOOK SO MUCH ALIKE that for a second I forget Henry is dead. I suck in my breath, repeating the truth to myself like a soothing mantra.

Henry Harris is dead, which means the man who just stepped onto this plane isn't my captor.

He can't be.

But he looks so much like him, from his unshaven face to his beer belly to that gaudy Hawaiian shirt.

Henry is dead, I tell myself. *Dead.* He can't hurt me anymore.

He can't reach me at all.

This man isn't Henry.

And then I see the girl traveling with him. The fear that looks so familiar behind her haunted eyes.

She doesn't belong with him.

I stare at the other passengers. Don't they see? Isn't someone going to do something? The flight attendants are cheerily helping people load the overhead bins and reminding folks to buckle up. Travelers are scrolling on their phones or reading books or shutting their eyes for a snooze.

Nobody else sees.

Nobody knows.

You're being paranoid, Anastasia, I tell myself. *Paranoid. That's all.*

Just because I happened to be abducted as a teen, just because a man named Henry who always wore Hawaiian shirts kept me locked up in his basement for two years so I could pretend to be his daughter — none of this means the girl I'm staring at is going through anything remotely similar.

She's wearing shorts and a T-shirt, which make her look even more out of place on this winter flight. Her eyes are puffy, outlined in dark rings. Maybe she's tired from a full day of travel. Or mad because her dad told her she had to break up with some deadbeat boyfriend. Or worried about her grandma who's lying on her deathbed in Detroit, praying that her family gets to see her one last time.

That's what I tell myself. That's what I have to believe if I'm not going to drive myself crazy.

"Miss Anastasia?"

"What is it?" I don't have the energy to remind Andrew to call me Mom. I haven't stopped staring at the girl. Begging God to give me some kind of sign to prove to me that she's okay.

"You stopped reading again," he complains.

"My throat's sore," I tell him. "I'm going to take a break."

My husband turns in his seat. Gives me one of his quiet smiles that always breaks my heart. Always makes me certain he's comparing me to her. Sometimes I want to yell in his face that I'm not his first wife and never will be, but what good would that accomplish?

Maybe we rushed into things too fast. Maybe Russel needed more time to grieve Sarah's death. More time to get himself ready for a new relationship. Looking back at how quickly our courtship progressed, I can't even speculate if he or I was the one who came across as the most desperate.

"You all right?" he asks me. I'm certain he's heard me being short with his son. Certain he's wondering why I can't be more soft-spoken, more tender-hearted, more maternal.

Why I can't be more like her.

I force a smile. "I'm good," I announce with such conviction the whole plane must believe me. "It's just a little loud in here. Makes it hard to read. My voice doesn't carry …" I let the words die on my lips. I'm staring again. Not at my husband. Not at this instant family I've somehow managed to make for myself.

But at her. This girl. She can't be more than fourteen or fifteen. Still a baby, really. Trusting of others because she hasn't learned yet how terrible life can be, how cruel the world can turn.

Happy because she doesn't know about Henry's basement. She hasn't been there yet. He hasn't taken her.

But he will.

My throat seizes shut. For a second, I

picture myself jumping out of my seat and demanding to be let off this plane. Running off, getting lost in the crowded airport. I'll write Russel an apology in a few weeks, once I've decided where I'm going to go, what I'm going to do. I'll apologize to the kids too. Tell them I'm so sorry, but I just can't be the kind of mommy they need.

But I don't. Instead, I sit here trembling in my seat. I'm buckled in, my family surrounding me. I have their snacks in my backpack, Betsy's pajamas thrown in too. There's nowhere for me to go. Nothing I can do except remember.

Remember the nightmare, the trauma, the terror. Remember everything I've tried so hard to run away from.

I've done a good job forgetting. At least, I thought I had. Thought I moved on.

When I didn't tell Russel about those two years in Henry's basement, it wasn't because I wanted to lie or mislead him. It was because in my foolishness, I actually believed I'd gotten over it. That my love for Russel and my newfound faith were enough to counteract my past, erase the trauma.

I felt so happy with Russel. So alive. I thought that meant I was finally healed …

That I could finally forget.

Except now, I remember. I sit here, trapped in this seat, my hands gripping the arm rests, the flight attendants still bustling back and forth to get everything ready for takeoff, and I remember everything.

SEVEN

HE SAYS his name is Henry Harris. "But you can call me Dad. Or Daddy. Whichever you prefer."

She tells him she wants to go home, and he lets out a soft chuckle. "This is your home, Jennifer."

She's already learned that she can't correct him. Can't tell him that her name is really Anastasia Reynolds, that she's never heard of Jennifer before and has no idea what happened to this poor daughter of his.

How long has she been here? It's hard to know because all the windows in this basement are boarded up. She's slept on and off, but has she been gone for hours or days? Could it be weeks?

At one point he knocked her unconscious. Her head hasn't felt quite right ever since. "You're lucky," he tells her after she wakes up. "It could have been a lot worse." He bandages a cut on the back of her head and says, his voice full of regret, "You remember what happened last time, don't you?"

She doesn't remember a last time because there never was a last time. Except she's smart enough not to tell Henry this. So instead she nods and lets him pet her blood-stained hair as he starts to cry and tell her how happy he is now that they're together again.

"You forgive me, don't you, Jennifer?" And she tells him that she does.

She learns to lie. As the basement grows colder and colder with the chill of winter, she begins to forget that there ever was a girl named Anastasia Reynolds. That there ever was a world outside of the cement prison, a world of snowflakes and ice skating and steaming hot chocolate fogging up her glasses while she takes dainty sips, careful not to burn her tongue.

She forgets that somewhere is a mother and a father desperate for her safe return, a mother and father who might even assume she's dead by now.

As long as they don't think she ran away ...

The cold that seeps into her soul becomes intolerable. She finds herself thankful for the nights when Henry can't sleep and brings down his blanket and joins her in the basement. Tells her stories about her childhood.

"Remember when Grandpa pitched you that softball and you broke the neighbor's window? He told you to go and apologize to the owners because he knew they couldn't be mad at a girl as cute and sweet as you. Remember that?"

And she tells him she does. Tells him so many times that every once in a while, she dreams about being that same little girl, standing on a doorstep she can recall in vivid detail, explaining to a tired-looking housewife that her grandpa was pitching and she accidentally broke their window.

Anastasia never played softball, but Jennifer did. Sometimes Henry even brings down the photo album and shows her pictures of her childhood. "That's your best friend, Shawna," he says. "She's living in

Chicago now, married to some big-time businessman. I saw her dad at the hardware store the other day. Says they're expecting their third kid. Isn't that great?"

And Anastasia feels somehow happy for Shawna, this best friend she never knew, this grown woman whose life has no resemblance to her own, this mother of three.

There are times when she wants to cry for Henry, when she looks at this pitiable old man, so alone, so lost in the past.

And there are times when she hates him. Hates what he's done to her. She's grown so skinny, she can feel her hips stabbing the cold cement floor at night when she tries to sleep. She hates the smell of his body odor but knows that she's even more unkempt than he is.

Some days, she's certain she could kill him.

Other days, she falls asleep crying, her heart aching for this lonely old man.

There's murmuring on the plane. My breath returns to me in a rush. I haven't had a flashback this vivid since … since … well, since long before I met Russel. That's why I was so sure I was doing better. So sure it wouldn't matter if I told him or not.

I stare at the middle-aged passenger ahead of me. He's in the aisle fidgeting with an overhead bag, and when he raises his arms his hairy stomach pokes out from beneath his Hawaiian shirt. I wonder for a minute how I could have ever confused him with Henry.

Henry wasn't that heavy for one thing. Not that hairy either. And this passenger is too young.

Besides, I remind myself, Henry is dead.

Henry is dead, so I have no reason to keep on thinking about him. No reason at all.

The children are getting restless. The flight attendant is shutting the last of the overhead compartments. That means we'll be taking off soon. Once we're in the air, I think I'll finally be able to relax.

I'm flying to Detroit. I'm going to meet my in-laws, going to spend a nice, relaxing vacation with them. The kids can't wait to see their grandma and grandpa, and Russel tells me that I'm going to get along just great with his sister. Life is good. I have everything I ever wanted, a husband who loves me, a strong and healthy family, the freedom to travel around and take time off to spend with relatives.

I'm safe. I'm healthy. And I can't let these scars from my past bubble to the surface and threaten everything I've got going for me right now.

EIGHT

"I DON'T WANT to read that one," Annie says.

"Me either," her brother grumbles.

I put the Grover book away and ask Andrew which one he'd like to choose.

He crosses his arms. "Something new," he says with a pout. "We've read all these before."

"Why don't you tell me a story?" I suggest, wondering if the impatience I'm feeling comes through my voice in spite of how hard I'm working to mask it.

"I don't know any stories," Andrew complains.

I'm at a loss. "Maybe your sister does," I finally suggest.

It's the only nudge little Annie needs, and in a second she's rattling off a tale of princesses and dragons in castles. Even with as sheltered as her father has kept her from contemporary movies and worldly influences, she sounds like any other child with the blessed gift of a fantastic imagination.

I fight my mind's urge to wander back, to take me again to Henry's basement. It's been years since I escaped. There's no way I'm going back. Never again. I'd sooner die.

"And then he tells Jennifer she's going to be his daughter forever and ever and ever."

My eyes widen. I feel the breath suck into my lungs as if a black hole has opened up in the space between my ribs. "What did you say?" I manage to stammer.

Annie gives me an annoyed look. She doesn't like to be interrupted.

"What did you say?" I repeat. I feel the blood emptying from my head, gushing to my extremities. For a minute, I have the terrible feeling that the man in the Hawaiian shirt is going to turn around in his seat and start laughing at me.

"I said that the princess and the prince lived happily ever after." Annie's voice is impatient, her lower lip protruding in an exaggerated pout.

"What did you say her name was?"

She's looking at me like I'm crazy. Am I? How can I know for sure?

"What was the princess's name?" I demand, leaning toward her.

"Jessie," Annie answers. "Weren't you listening?"

"I thought you said her name was Jennifer," I mumble. Suddenly exhausted, I slump back into my seat.

"It's *Jessie*," Annie states with all the authority of a four-year-old who's entirely sure of herself.

"And who was it that wanted to be her dad?"

"What?" Her eyes are wide, and now both Annie and her brother are staring at me as if my hair has just turned green.

"You said the bad guy told the princess she had to be his daughter for ever and ever."

Annie contorts her face. I can't quite gauge her emotion. Is it confusion? Disgust?

"That was the *prince*," she tells me with an exasperated huff. "The prince said,

'You'll be my wife for ever and ever.' Didn't you hear that part?"

"Sorry," I answer distractedly. I feel my throat constrict, sense my hands gripping the arm rests of my seat, feel the seatbelt prodding into my stomach. It's too tight, but I can't loosen it. I shut my eyes, and I'm back in the basement, a scared little girl whose only dream is to go home.

A victim who's rage and quest for vengeance is the only incentive she has left to stay alive.

NINE

Jennifer applied her roll-on deodorant and frowned at the mirror. Her bangs had been hanging a little limp ever since she got home from school.

Nothing some extra hair spray couldn't solve.

Dad knocked on her door. He was in a hurry, like always, but she wasn't ready yet.

"Jennifer?" he called to her. "You done in there?"

"In a minute." She picked up her brush and pretended it was a microphone and she was on stage belting out the melody with Boyz II Men. She practiced a few dance moves in front of the mirror. Would this be the night Darren would ask her to dance?

She sprayed her bangs again, then spritzed more mousse onto the palm of her hand before scrunching up her curls in hopes of giving them a little extra bounce.

It had taken a lot of pleading to convince her dad to let her go out tonight. She could swear it sometimes felt like her dad's one goal in life was to keep her trapped as a prisoner in her own home. If he could handcuff her and keep her locked up in the basement, she sometimes wondered if he would.

Well, tonight was going to be different. It was her first school dance. Darren would be there. All of her friends. It was just this year that Lisa and some of the other popular girls had started paying attention to her. Tonight was her chance to prove she truly fit into their group. She'd been practicing her moves in front of the mirror, sneaking in snippets of that dance show on MTV every morning, studying the dancers until she knew the right way to move her body.

Darren was going to be so impressed. She hoped he'd ask her to slow dance with him. Especially if a Boyz II Men song came on. He knew she loved Boyz II Men.

Dad pounded on the door again. Jennifer applied one more layer of lipliner, gave herself a last once-over in the mirror, and stepped out of her room.

She felt like a princess about to attend her very first ball. No, that was too childish. She was like those dancers on MTV, the ones who always looked perfect and were always surrounded by admirers. This was her night. Her time to make a lasting impression, not only on Darren but on Lisa and all her friends and their entire freshman class.

This was Jennifer's time to shine.

TEN

She got out of the house without Dad grumbling much about her clothes. She'd already planned out each and every one of her arguments if he said her skirt was too short or her top was too tight, but he was surprisingly quiet when he drove her to the school.

"Drop me off here," she said a block away from the bus stop. Behind them, a car sped by.

"Let me off here," she repeated, more urgently when she started to fear her dad might actually drive her up to the school itself. What if Darren was here? What if he saw her getting dropped off? She had her hand on the door and was willing to roll out of the Chevy before it stopped, but Dad finally slowed down to let her out.

"Don't pick me up until 9:30," she told him, slamming the door shut before he could make any last arguments or change his mind about allowing her out tonight. It wasn't really her dad's fault he was like this. He'd been overly protective of her for years, ever since Mom died. Jennifer understood. It didn't make his behavior any more bearable, but at least she knew he meant well.

"Oh, my gosh, is that you, Jennifer?" She recognized Lisa's voice in an instant, her heart skipping a slight beat to have been noticed. "Look at your hair! It's so curly."

Jennifer beamed and joined the circle of Lisa's friends, who were making their way toward the school. When they stepped into the gym, the girls congealed into one massive, dancing throng in the middle of the crowd. Jennifer scrunched up her curls, hoping they'd keep their volume all night, hoping her deodorant would work, hoping this dance would be just as perfect as she imagined.

A familiar beat came over the speakers,

and Lisa grabbed her by the wrist. "Come on!" she shouted. "Macarena!"

And in an instant, Jennifer forgot how worried she'd been about her hair, her deodorant, her dad. She forgot about how desperately she wanted her friends at school to like her, to include her, to treat her like one of them. She forgot everything except for the music. The beat washed over her worries, drowned out her fears. She knew this dance, even though she'd never done it with a group this large before. Everyone moved at the exact same time, following the exact same script, one living being whose parts moved together in perfect unity.

She had never felt so happy before. Never so alive before. Like she'd been made for this moment, to dance here to this song at this precise instant in time. Lisa, the most popular girl in the ninth-grade class, was on her left, and they were surrounded by the coolest, prettiest girls in school. There was only one thing that would make tonight even more perfect.

Jennifer was lightheaded when the song ended. A few boys groaned when a slow song came on. Jennifer held her breath. The

DJ was playing Boyz II Men already? It was too soon. Darren wasn't here. At least she hadn't seen him yet …

Shawna and Kylee, Lisa's two best friends, stared at Jennifer and began to giggle. They leaned over to whisper in one another's ears. What was going on?

And then she felt it. The tap on her shoulder. The electric spark zinging down her arm and throughout her entire body.

Darren.

"Wanna dance?"

It was impossible to remember the exact order of what happened next. Did he put her hands on her waist, or did she say yes to him first? Was she the one who took a step closer, or was that him?

"The thing about slow dancing is it's like you're giving him a five-minute hug." That's what someone had written in to *Teen* magazine for their article on your first school dance. And as it turned out, the author was exactly right.

"You like Boyz II Men, don't you?" Darren asked.

Jennifer could hardly hear his words over the pounding of her heart, the swell of the music. "Yeah," she answered, only then piecing the individual words he spoke to her together to try to form some kind of meaning out of them.

And he pulled her closer. Her feet were touching his. Each time he swayed, she swayed, and the music wrapped them up in a warm cloud of perfect bliss.

It was even more perfect than she'd been dreaming.

"Thanks," Darren said, grinning at her. Why had he stopped moving?

Jennifer's face flushed. She hadn't even heard the song end. She wasn't sure what was supposed to happen next. Was she supposed to say thank you back? Was she supposed to tell him you're welcome? Or maybe she was supposed to grab his hand right there and make sure everyone around them knew that she'd be dancing with Darren and Darren only for the rest of the night.

She was still trying to decide what to do, terrified of saying the wrong thing, thinking back desperately to that article in *Teen* to remember if they'd given any kind of rules. How do you end a slow dance?

"Thank you," she finally managed to stammer, but Darren had already disappeared.

Shawna and Kylee pounced on her an instant later. "Oh, my gosh. Did you seriously just dance with him? You two looked adorable. Are you going out?"

"When did Darren start to notice someone like you?" And then Lisa stepped up to their group, her face not so excited, her smile not so friendly. Shawna and Kylee backed away. Jennifer could feel their eyes on her. Wait, why were they upset? She hadn't done anything wrong, had she?

"Was that Darren you were dancing with?" Lisa's voice had a grainy edge to it that made Jennifer want to cover her ears.

She tried to laugh. "Yeah, crazy, right? He just came up and started dancing." Was that how it happened? Jennifer couldn't even remember. They were playing a rap song now, but it felt like her feet were still swaying slowly, like they were still pressed up against Darren's as their bodies moved together in perfect rhythm.

"Cute, Jennifer." Lisa flipped her hair over her shoulder. She'd straightened it for tonight. Jennifer suddenly felt juvenile and fake with her bouncy curls and took a step back.

"Cute," Lisa repeated.

Jennifer glanced at Shawna and Kylee to see if she could pick up any clues from them. What was going on? They circled around Lisa, giggling, and the trio turned their backs on Jennifer and walked away.

What was that all about?

The very next song was another slow one. Jennifer didn't recognize it. She glanced around the gym, wondering where Darren was, if he'd come up from behind and tap her on the shoulder again like before. Or maybe she'd see him first, smile, and walk straight up to him.

She inched her way toward the walls as couples took over the center of the gym. They looked so awkward together, some of them standing with a full foot of separation between them. Not like Jennifer and Darren, where she'd been pressed so close to him she was certain he could feel her heart thudding against his chest.

Where was he?

And then she saw. Lisa was talking to him, her hand on her hip, her body at an angle. Her two best friends stood on either side of her like guards, their arms crossed, their faces set in scowls. Darren looked helpless. He looked … Wait, what was going on?

Lisa's posture relaxed. She slunk up toward him, putting her hands on his shoulders. On Darren's shoulders. That's not what was supposed to happen.

Shawna and Kylee grinned when his hands circled around Lisa's tiny waist. Her hair was so long now that it was straight it fell past the small of her back. Somebody bumped into Jennifer. She thought she heard someone asking her a question, but her mind refused to work. Her body refused to move.

What was Darren doing?

Shawna and Kylee turned and looked straight at her. Did they know she'd been here watching them this whole time?

Jennifer wanted to turn and run away, but she couldn't. Not when Darren was there, dancing with the most popular girl in ninth grade. Lisa with her straightened hair. Why had Jennifer decided to scrunch up her curls tonight, anyway? She looked ridiculous. Like a poodle in a dog show.

Shawna and Kylee grinned as they stepped up to her. "Hey, Jennifer, can we talk to you outside?" Shawna asked.

Jennifer still hadn't stopped staring at Darren. There were dozens, maybe hundreds of students in between them, but their eyes locked for a split second.

He gave a shy smile and an embarrassed shrug. Then he rested his cheek on Lisa's gorgeous, straightened hair as he swayed with her in perfect time to the music.

ELEVEN

"Yeah, so here's the thing." Shawna jutted out her hip, just like Jennifer had seen Lisa do a dozen times a day. Next to her, standing just behind Shawna's shoulder, Kylee twirled her straight hair around her pointer finger and chewed loudly on her bubble gum.

"So, Darren's gonna ask Lisa out tonight," Shawna said, never once taking her eyes off Jennifer. "And, well, we know you like him."

"Yeah," Kylee inserted. "It's totally obvious."

Jennifer ignored the burning in her cheeks. She shouldn't feel embarrassed. She should feel angry. What was this? Some kind of interrogation in the girls' bathroom?

The toilet from one of the stalls flushed, and the three of them were silent as a gangly girl hurried out, not even bothering to wash her hands.

Shawna and Kylee followed her out with their eyes.

"Gross," Shawna hissed.

"I know," Kylee whispered back.

Jennifer was relieved to no longer be the center of their focus. Unfortunately, the reprieve lasted only a second or two.

"So, anyway," Shawna went on, "Lisa asked us to tell you to stop hanging all over Darren, if you know what we mean."

Kylee smacked her gum loudly and added a very emphatic, "Yeah."

"Because you're kind of embarrassing yourself the way you're all over him and everything."

Shawna and Kylee laughed. Jennifer took a step back.

"We don't want to hurt your feelings," Shawna concluded, "but Darren's already told Adam and Russ and Craig that he likes Lisa better. We just wanted you to know so you could stop acting all weird around him.

No offense, but people are starting to talk about you."

Kylee gave a little snicker. Jennifer wished that she could conjure up a spell to make the floor open up and swallow her whole.

She didn't hear what Shawna and Kylee said next. She hardly even noticed them walk out and leave her in the bathroom alone. She reached into her pocket, counted out her change. Down the hill from the school was a pay phone. Maybe her dad was right. Maybe these dances were nothing but a big waste of time.

Whatever happened, she wasn't going back into that gym. Not with Darren acting like such a two-timing player, not with Lisa standing there with her arms draped all over him. It was either call her dad, walk home in the dark, or stay here in the bathroom.

Jennifer allowed herself the luxury of a short cry locked inside one of the stalls, then she counted her coins again and made her way down the hill.

It was time to call her dad.

TWELVE

THE FLIGHT ATTENDANT made one more announcement, another apology for the few minutes' delay. We're not in the air yet. The door to the gate isn't even closed. I could get off now. Pretend like I need to use the bathroom in the front of the plane, then walk away and never look back …

Except I know I can't do that. At least, I know I shouldn't do that. When I became a Christian, Russel assured me that God freed me from the sins of my past. That means I don't have to be terrified anymore, do I?

I wonder if Russel would have told me those same comforting platitudes if he knew who I really am.

I stare down the aisle, stare at that open door as if it's my last connection to safety. If those attendants shut that gate, if I just sit here and fly out to Detroit and meet my in-laws and accept all their profuse congratulations for my marriage to Russel, I'm stuck in this life, in this skirt, in this headscarf for good.

I'm not who any of them think I am, but if I allow myself to stay here on this plane, I'm going to wake up one day and realize there's no more me left at all.

I had a dream right after Russel proposed. I was her. Sarah, his first wife. I was wearing her clothes, cooking meals in her kitchen, homeschooling her kids, tending her garden. The children called me Mom. Even Russel called me by her name.

When I looked in the mirror, it wasn't my own face that I saw. It was hers. Pale and tired and wrapped up in that old-fashioned kerchief. I felt like I'd stepped out of an 1860s frontier TV show. Is this what I am? A mail-order bride escaping the dangers of the city to hedge my bets and do what I can to make life work out in the untamed wilderness?

I woke up crying. I hadn't done that in years. My pajamas were drenched in sweat, my cheeks soaked with tears. I don't want to be Sarah. I don't want to pretend. But if Russel knew the truth …

I can't do that to him. Not after he's trusted me with his love, his kids. He's flying us out to Detroit to introduce me to his parents, for goodness sake. It's because of Russel I have a roof over my head. I have food to eat. It's because of Russel I know who Jesus is. When I ran away from my past, I wasn't looking for spiritual awakening, but God brought it to me anyway.

And he used this man who loves me, the man I pledged to love and honor and cherish until death do us part. Russel has already started the paperwork for me to adopt his kids. It will be my name on their new birth certificates, as if Sarah never even existed.

I'm sweating. I'm shaking. I'm biting my lip until I'm certain I'm about to draw blood.

"Are you ready to hear what happens next?" The tiny voice beside me has grown familiar but still sounds so strange. How can

I pretend that this child is my own, that I can ever be a fraction of the mother that she needs?

"What happens next?" I ask, still keeping my eyes on the front of the plane. They haven't shut the doors yet. There's still time …

"So the prince tells the princess that he wants to be married to her and live together for ever and ever in their great big castle, and he's going to keep her locked up in the basement for the rest of her life."

I snap my focus away from the front of the plane to stare at my stepdaughter. "He did what?" I demand. I hope her father hasn't overheard. If so, he'll think I'm the one filling her head with scary images of kidnappings and torture.

"I said he kept the wicked witch locked in the dungeon." Annie pauses with a pout before finally adding, "That's the end."

I feel the breath return to my lungs, repeat the words I just heard her say. *He kept the wicked witch locked in the dungeon.* I don't remember a wicked witch in the story, but I assume she got what was coming to her all along.

"That sounds like a very good ending," I

say, but even I'm not convinced by my own words. I repeat them, more forcefully this time, and the captain gets on to tell the flight attendants to prepare the cabin for departure.

THIRTEEN

Dad was in a foul mood by the time he rolled in to pick Jennifer up at the bottom of the hill. If she'd known he'd be this late, she would have started walking instead of standing in the cold like an absolute idiot. What was her dad thinking, leaving her out alone like this?

She was glad when they got home. Glad when Dad sauntered into his room and slammed the door shut instead of yelling or telling her how dumb she was for wanting to go to a school dance in the first place.

The truth was humiliating to admit, but Dad had been right all along. Dances were stupid.

The *Teen* magazine she'd been studying

all month lay open on her bed. She ripped out the pages about school dances and flung the shreds into the trash. Too bad their home didn't have a fireplace. She would have liked to watch the pieces burn.

Hot tears streamed down her cheeks by the time she saw her eighth-grade yearbook on her nightstand. She yanked the cover open. She hadn't realized it before, but Darren and Lisa's pictures were just one row apart from each other.

She ripped out the entire page, crumbling it to a ball, wishing there was something else she could do to give voice to her rage. She turned to the page where she knew she'd find Shawna's photograph when she heard something at her window. At first she ignored it. The wind had picked up. She couldn't let herself get interrupted by every little sound that made her jump. She had a job to do.

Out with Shawna's smiling face. Another page to crumble up. Maybe Jennifer should have drawn on the picture first. Given Shawna and Lisa and all of them the hideous makeovers they all deserved.

The humiliating conversation from the

bathroom ran unchecked through Jennifer's mind.

You're kind of embarrassing yourself the way you're all over him and everything.

Jennifer gave a roar as she ripped Kylee's face out of the yearbook then paused to see if her dad had overheard. Most likely, he'd already fallen asleep, but she didn't want to wake him up with her yelling.

She strained her ears, fearing the sound of her father's door opening down the hallway. Then she heard it again. A tapping outside her window. Either the wind had really picked up or …

She froze when she saw the flashlight beaming in through the glass. What was going on?

Another rapping. Was it Darren? He knew where she lived, didn't he? They rode the bus together through all of middle school. Even though she thought she'd been totally invisible to him at the time, he could find a way to remember that much, right?

She wiped the tears from her face then yanked up the blinds. It felt just like in the TV shows. Darren at her window, come to apologize.

Except it wasn't Darren.

"Shawna?" Jennifer couldn't remember the last time she'd talked to Shawna without Kylee in arm's reach. It felt strange to see her alone.

"I came to apologize," Shawna said, smoothing out her hair. "I didn't see you at the dance and thought you might be upset. There's a party going on at Kylee's house. I wanted to know if you'd come with me." She paused and lowered her eyes. "I'm really sorry about what we said to you. You know we didn't mean it. Wanna come?"

Jennifer glanced at the clock on her desk then at her closed door. If her dad found her sneaking out like this, he'd kill her. She thought about how silent and withdrawn he'd been since Mom died. How he could spend weeks hardly leaving his room. How protective he'd gotten of Jennifer. How worried he'd be if he found her gone.

Jennifer was about to fake a sore throat when Shawna lay her hand against the screen. "Come on. Basically everybody's going to be there."

Jennifer held her breath. A real party? And Shawna came all this way to invite her?

Jennifer looked at the clock once more. Kylee's house wasn't too far away. She could go for just a short time and be right back. Her dad would never know.

Shawna gave a sly smile. "Darren'll be there," she added.

Jennifer turned back once more to find her shoes and told Shawna she was ready to go.

FOURTEEN

DARREN HADN'T LEFT her side all night. Jennifer had promised herself to leave Kylee's by eleven, but it was nearly midnight, and she was no closer to going home than she'd been when she first arrived.

"Isn't your dad going to get mad if he finds out you're here?" Darren asked. He had a dimple in his right cheek when he smiled.

And he'd been smiling the entire time he and Jennifer had been talking.

Jennifer didn't like the fact that everyone in her school seemed to know how protective her father was, so she gave a convincing laugh and shrugged. "What he doesn't know can't hurt him, right?"

Darren laughed too, a confident, easy laugh. Jennifer wasn't sure she'd ever been as relaxed and happy as he appeared to be right now as they sat side by side in Kylee's living room.

"I looked for you at the dance," he said in a low voice. Jennifer couldn't be certain, but she thought he leaned toward her an inch. His hand was so close to hers, a small twitch and their fingers would be touching.

"I, um, I had to leave early." She hated herself as soon as the words escaped her mouth. Why couldn't she have come up with something else to say? She cleared her throat and forced as massive a smile as she could manage. "What did you think, though? Did you have fun?"

"It was all right," he answered. "I would have had even more fun if you were there the whole time." He inched toward her again. His leg brushed against hers, or maybe that was just part of his pants. Jennifer was afraid to breathe. What if he could sense how nervous she was? What if she had bad breath? Why hadn't she thought to add more deodorant before she sneaked out of the house and ran off with Shawna?

His pinky finger moved subtly. What was

that? Was he trying to hold her hand? Sending her some kind of secret signal? She'd never held hands with a boy before. What if he took her hand now and it was all sweaty? What would he think?

She moved her hand and wiped her palm on the couch cushion. Darren looked down for a minute. Had she hurt his feelings? Did he think she was turning him down? She had to think of something to say, something fast.

"Dad hasn't really been the same since Mom died." And right there, Jennifer wished that she could disappear into the floor. It was as if the magic she'd been pretending to live under — here with Darren, him paying attention to her and only her — was a spell she'd just destroyed by bringing up such a depressing topic. She had to think fast, had to make it right, had to correct her mistake.

"Yeah, that really sucks," he replied before she could say anything else.

She couldn't breathe. Darren was staring into her eyes. He didn't laugh at her. Didn't get up and walk away. Didn't abandon her to go find Lisa, who was so much prettier and cooler than Jennifer could ever hope to be. He didn't do any of those things.

Jennifer gave a half-hearted chuckle. "Yeah. It kinda does."

And they both laughed and started talking about Mr. Green, the science teacher back in middle school who was rumored to smoke marijuana on a daily basis. Half the girls at their school secretly had a crush on him, and there was no end to making fun of the ones who made the biggest fools of themselves to win his attention.

It was past midnight now. Jennifer knew she'd have to go home soon. She hadn't meant to stay nearly this long to begin with. But she'd lost all sense of time with Darren by her side, their legs pressed up against each other, his pinky inching close to hers before pulling away so subtly she sometimes feared she imagined it.

Kylee's stereo had already started to reshuffle its playlist. Only a few kids were left. Kylee wanted them all to come outside so she could show off the new hot tub in the back yard, and for a fragment of an eternity, Jennifer and Darren were in the living room completely alone.

He'd been telling her about what it was like spending summers with his dad when everything stopped. The din of the crowd.

The song on the CD player. The pulse of Jennifer's heart.

Their eyes locked. She couldn't have looked away from him if her life depended on it.

And then his hand was on hers. Not just touching and slipping away. He was grasping her hand now, and all of a sudden, she didn't care how sweaty her palms were.

And in that instant she knew. She knew that he would have never told Adam or Russ or Craig that Lisa was prettier. Would have never preferred to dance with Lisa. Jennifer thought back to the scene in the gym. He'd wanted to be with her. That's why he gave her that look, that shrug. Lisa had grabbed him, demanded a slow dance, and he was too kind-hearted to turn her down. Shawna and Kylee and Lisa were all jealous. That was all there was too it. Jealous of Jennifer because Darren liked her.

Darren chose her.

Darren wanted her.

She held her breath, certain that if she opened her mouth just a little her heart would leap up out of her throat. That's exactly when it happened. The tiniest of kisses, the kind that wouldn't have even counted in any other situation. He missed her lips but grazed the corner of her mouth. A quick motion, not quite a peck but definitely something. Something real.

He pulled away. She tried to think of something to say. Anything to say. What do you say at a time like this?

She realized her hand was still in his. He hadn't pulled it away.

She stood up. She had to think of something to do. Had to make it sound like this sort of thing happened to her every single day. Darren could never know that she'd never been kissed before, never held hands before, never been so in love in her entire life before. She just had to act cool. Natural.

Piece of cake.

"Wanna see the hot tub?" Darren's voice gave a little squeak. Jennifer stared at her feet.

"I should get home," she said. "It's … my dad … It's getting late …"

She raised her eyes once, let them flicker up to his face. Was he blushing?

She wiped her palm on the side of her pants. "Thank you," she stammered and hoped that he wouldn't ask what he was thanking her for, because she wouldn't have the slightest clue how to respond.

Darren cleared his throat. "Yeah, um, thanks to you too. I mean, have a good night. I mean, yeah."

Jennifer couldn't suppress her giggle. "Okay. Yeah. Bye."

He scratched at his neck. Shifted his weight from side to side. He called something out after her, but she was already racing toward the front door, her feet flying, her heart soaring into the stratosphere.

She was halfway down the driveway when a low, menacing voice made her stop in her tracks.

"So this is where you've been."

FIFTEEN

"I HAVE TO GET OFF," I'm telling my husband. The moment the pilot told the attendants to shut the doors, I knew. Knew there was no way I could go through with this. No way I could continue on to Detroit.

"What's gotten into you?" Russel's voice is firm. I know I'm making a scene, but I can't help it. I haven't felt this trapped in years, not since I found myself in Henry's basement.

I was fifteen, even though he insisted I was a full year younger. I told him my name was Anastasia, I begged him to let me tell my parents I was okay, but he wouldn't listen to me.

"Your name is Jennifer," he said. "You're my sweet little pineapple. We're finally together, just like we were supposed to be."

I tried running away. After the first few weeks of compliance, he finally took the cuffs off. The very next morning I made it halfway up the basement steps before he stopped me, tackled me to the floor. I went days without food as my punishment.

I complain. Tell him how my stomach hurts.

"You've always been worried about being overweight," Henry tells me. "I'm doing you a favor."

I cry then, tell him I'm sorry about whatever it was that happened to his daughter, but I don't know anything about anyone named Jennifer and won't he please let me go.

It's talks like this that earn me starvation rations. More beatings. Endless nights chained up in the basement, an animal in a cage. An animal he insists on calling Jennifer, his daughter.

The weeks wear on. The cold seeps into my bones. I'm ashamed to admit it. Maybe I should have been stronger. I go along with his games. I call him Daddy like he wants. Every time he begs for my forgiveness, I give it to him, even though I have no idea what he's sorry for.

"They came every day, questioning me," Henry says. His voice is so full of sadness I want to cry for him, for his poor little girl, whoever she was, for his loss.

I don't ask him what happened to Jennifer. I'm not sure I want to know.

"Once your mother died, I thought I couldn't go on," he says one night. He's recently cracked one of my ribs, and now he's rubbing some kind of salve on my skin. It stings, but the touch is gentle. His voice is kind but filled with heaviness.

"I begged God to put me out of my misery," he admits. "I didn't want to live anymore, not without her. But I had you. You're the one who kept me going. You're the one who kept me alive." There's a hint of pride in his voice, and I'm so tired and so homesick and so confused that for a minute I wish that I really was this man's daughter. That I really could ease his sorrow, heal the wounds of his past just like he's healing the wounds in my side.

I forget how long I've been here now. Long enough that I don't think of my captor as Henry. I call him Dad, and at night when I dream, I'm his daughter.

Sometimes I ask him what day it is, but I can never keep his answers straight in my head. And sometimes I know he deliberately lies to me, like during that heat wave he told me it was still March. We celebrated my birthday in the fall. Jennifer's birthday, I should say, although these days it's hard for me to remember that there's a difference.

"It's the anniversary of your accident," he tells me one day. I don't like it when he talks about the accident, when he hints to the tragedy that befell his daughter.

When Henry first brought me here, when he kept apologizing to me and telling me I was Jennifer and he was so sickeningly sorry for what happened, I was convinced he'd killed her.

"They kept questioning me after it happened," Henry says to me nearly every day.

At first when he talked like this, I wondered why the police didn't do more than just question him, why they didn't put him in prison to rot for the rest of his miserable existence. I imagined he must have killed her. Strangled her maybe. Or beat her with a bat. But now, it's hard for me to picture him doing anything to Jennifer like that. He has a temper on him, but he acts so gentle. He's old now. Weak. Sometimes he stops in the middle of whatever he's doing to me simply because he's out of breath and needs to rest.

He likes me to soak his feet in salts. The skin on his heels is hardened and cracking all over, and he likes it when I massage them in warm water. When he's done, I pat them dry and rub in lotion.

"You're such a good daughter," he tells me, and my heart aches because somewhere I remember I have a father who used to say the same thing to me, but it's been so long I can hardly recall the sound of his voice. Sometimes I feel like I've been living in Henry's basement for decades, that my whole life has consisted of nothing but his rage, his pity, his love.

He's worn me down. I don't fight anymore. The truth is I don't want to. I'm too tired. When he gets angry, I remember that somewhere is a dead teenager who must have looked and acted and least somewhat like me for Henry to have gotten the two of us so confused. I remember that at some point Henry did something terrible to her, that she's gone, dead, and Henry is a broken man because of it.

I believe he's responsible for Jennifer's murder, and that means he could kill me too. The thought comes to me most often in the middle of the night, when I hear him snoring upstairs. If this man could murder his own daughter and get away with it, why in the world do I think myself safe?

Except what can I do? Everything's locked. Even though he hardly ever uses the handcuffs anymore, there's no place for me to run. Nothing I can do. When he's awake, when he's in one of those fits of rage that overcome him, I'm quite certain that he not only possesses the strength to kill me but the will as well. Sometimes I wonder why he doesn't just get it over with already. I wish for it at times. Intentionally egg him on. There's very little left for me to fight for. I don't want to hurt anymore. That's all I know. And life with Henry is a life of pain. Not the physical so much as the mental. The emotional. The sadness, the regret, the remorse, everything he feels about his daughter — all that grief and anguish — I take it upon myself, just like after I've finished rubbing lotion into his scaly heels my own hands are drenched in oil.

I think we've become inseparable, Henry and me. I think if I were to leave it would kill him. Is that why I stay? Or do I stay because of the chains, the locks, the fear? And in the end, if I'm destined to die here in this cement basement one way or the other, does it really matter?

At night, I dream about my mother. I dream that she's at home praying for my safety. I try to tell her I'm all right, that she can move on, that she doesn't have to worry anymore. I try to promise her that I'll fight harder next time, that one day I'll manage to escape and return to her, heal her broken heart. But she can never hear me, and when I wake up, I realize that I've forgotten the details of her face. I can't recall her smell, the sound of her making breakfast in the kitchen in the morning.

All I see is Henry. All I hear is Henry. He's become my life, just like I've become his.

I forget about the promises I make to my

mother in my dreams. I forget about a world outside of this cold basement. And I massage my father's feet and lotion his dry skin and take his pain upon myself because he's old and weak and needs me to ease the intolerable anguish in his soul.

SIXTEEN

"What do you want me to do?" Russel asks. "We're about to take off."

"I'm sorry about your parents," I say. "But I can't do this. I need to get off."

Russel looks at me as if I've started speaking gibberish. I want to make him understand, but how can I? He doesn't know who I am. He doesn't know what I've done. He doesn't realize that I never should have married him in the first place, not with all the secrets I've kept from him. The truth is I can't make this trip with him to Detroit. Can't meet his parents. I can't keep on pretending.

I glance at the man ahead of me, the one in the Hawaiian shirt, the one that for a moment I was convinced was a younger ver-sion of Henry. If I keep seeing images of my captor every time I'm out in public, how am I supposed to lead anything resembling a normal life?

I need to get myself back home, back to the quiet of Russel's farm. Actually, I don't care where I go, but I know I can't stay here.

Russel needs an explanation. He's not the sort of person who goes by gut instinct, who lets himself be driven by fear or emo-tions. I've got to give him an actual reason, something he can accept even if he can't understand.

Even if I have to lie.

"I don't think it's safe," I blurt out. It isn't exactly what I meant to say, but I realize as soon as the words leave my mouth that they'll serve their purpose nicely. "It's not safe," I repeat, lowering my voice.

Russel still isn't ready to let me walk off this flight, so I play the women's intuition card, hoping it'll be enough. "I have a really bad feeling about this," I say, keeping my voice low.

In a flash, I see the next five minutes playing out perfectly in my head. Russel tells me I'm being ridiculous, that we're totally fine, that his parents are waiting for us in Detroit. Then I get up anyway, tell the flight attendant I'm demanding to get off this plane.

I give Annie a quick hug. Out of all the children, I'll miss her the most. I don't look back to see Russel's pained face, because even though he might not be quite as intuitive as some, he'll understand, he'll realize that I'm not just giving up on this flight.

I'm giving up on this dream, this ridiculous notion that with all of our differences and the secrets of my past we can actually make this marriage work.

Except that's not what happens. I watched wide-eyed as my husband takes a deep breath, looks at his kids, sighs once more, then signals the flight attendant.

"I'm sorry to cause trouble," he says when she walks up to check on us, "but I need to get my family off this flight. Now."

SEVENTEEN

I KNOW that everyone is staring at us as we walk down the aisle to get off the plane. The children are confused. I have no idea what I'm going to tell them. I have no idea what I'm going to tell Russel.

We pass the man in the Hawaiian shirt. My skin bristles. I feel dirty and exposed just being within arm's reach. I hold my breath, as if the air surrounding him might somehow be contaminated. It was the same way I used to hold my breath when I'd hear Henry coming down the stairs first thing in the morning. I was never certain if he'd be in a good mood or not.

I've read a few articles about women who've survived the kinds of things I have. A lot of them talk about how important it was to get therapy after what they'd been through. I never saw a therapist myself. Couldn't stand the thought of sitting in front of some stranger reliving everything … everything …

I actually haven't told anyone the full truth.

I learned to hide the emotion, at times even from myself, but my hatred and loathing for Henry grew with each passing day of my captivity. It's hard to imagine now that I could despise him so much and still ache for his pain. Still mourn his tragic family life. I don't pretend to understand how or why it turned out that way, but that's what happened.

I had no idea two full years had passed since my kidnapping. I'd lost track of time. Didn't know if I'd been in Henry's basement for four months or four decades. It all felt exactly the same to me.

It was the day I finally learned the truth about what happened to Henry's daughter. I'd grown so used to Jennifer's disappearance being such a mystery, I think I actually forgot sometimes that Henry was mourning the loss of a real flesh-and-blood human being and not some phantom he'd created in his mind.

"You snuck out of the house that night," he tells me. There's something strange in his voice. I don't think he's drunk, but there's something not quite right. Sometimes he calls me Jennifer, and other times he talks about her as if we're separate people and always have been.

"I would have let you go if you asked me." His voice is so pained my heart feels like it's going to bleed dry. "I would have driven you to make sure you got there safely."

I know he doesn't really expect me to answer him back, so I simply sit and listen. I'm not thinking about his daughter. I'm not thinking about how strange it is that he's finally decided to talk about what happened to her after all this time I've been with him. I'm thinking about how sad he sounds, about how desperately I'd like to find a way to make him smile. To ease his pain.

"She was stubborn. There was a boy there that she liked." The words jog a distant memory, the vaguest of notions that at one point I also was a teenage girl who had crushes and went out to parties and did things I hoped my parents would never find out about.

"You were beat up pretty bad." He's staring at me now, but there's something strange in his eyes, like he's not really looking at me at all. I feel exposed. Vulnerable. For a second, I want to ask him to stop, but then I think that maybe if he gets the rest of this story off his chest, it'll finally bring him the relief we've been searching for.

"I went out looking for you. I searched everywhere. And there you were, in the woods behind your old school. I swear I didn't lay a finger on you. It wasn't me, but they wouldn't believe me. Police asked me all kinds of questions. Why I went out looking for you myself instead of calling 911. Why two girls said they saw me pick Jennifer up from that party even though I said she ran away. Why I couldn't show them the next day exactly where it was I'd found you so they could test the crime scene themselves. Why I brought you home and didn't think to take you to a hospital right away. I had no idea the injuries were that bad. She was in bad shape, Jennifer was, but I thought she was drunk. Heaven and everything blessed forgive me, but I thought she was drunk and that's why she was so floppy in my arms. Kids do that, you know. Teens do that. But they did an autopsy and there wasn't a drop of alcohol in your system, my little pineapple. I'm sorry I ever even suspected you. You hadn't been drinking, but I didn't know that. I thought you just needed to come home. I thought you needed to sleep it off."

Henry's voice is cracking, and my heart aches so much it's decided to hold still. I can't erase the words you say next. Can't stop you when you start to cry.

"The next morning, I wanted to let you sleep in. By the time I started to get worried, you were cold. Heaven help me if it's not the blessed truth. You were already cold. I called 911 right away then. Screamed at them to get me an ambulance. Begged them to help you, but they couldn't. It was too late by then. But that wasn't all. It was bad enough losing you. Then everyone thought I'm the one who did it. I was in a bad way after Jennifer's mother died. Lost my job. Didn't function too great. One doctor said I had an illness in my brain, but he was a quack.

"I'd gotten angry with you before. I guess you even told the school counselor you were worried for me. You had every right to tell her those things, by the way, and I've never blamed you, but by heaven that counselor took your words and twisted them and told the police that you were scared of me. Can you believe it? Scared of me. And they couldn't understand how if it happened the way I said it happened that I could have just put you in bed to die. Heaven help me, Jennifer, but I swear I had no idea you were that bad off. You'll never forgive me, but you have to know how sorry I am. I love you so much, pineapple. I've never stopped loving you."

And something clicks in my head right then. Memories of home, of love, of my parents. It's like I've been living under a shadow and the spell is finally broken.

I look at Henry, who's begging me to believe him, whose cries have turned into sobs, and I wake up from a two-year-long hypnosis.

"I believe you," I say, gritting my jaw because I truly want to gag on the words. "I know you didn't mean to do it." Except I'm lying to him. For the first time in Henry's basement, I feel like my brain is working clearly. Call it survival instinct, or maybe it was the answer to all my mother's prayers, but I realize now that I've been duped by a crazy man.

A man who's not only crazy but a murderer.

"I believe you," I repeat, even though I've put the pieces together to know exactly what happened to Henry's daughter so many years ago. The way he talks about it, the way he lets things slip out, this bizarre explanation he's trying to get me to believe, I can read through the lines and finally know what happened.

Jennifer sneaked away from home. That part's true enough. She went to a party, probably flirted with that boy Henry mentioned she liked. And the rest is easy to piece together. Henry realized what she'd done. Either he went looking for her himself or waited until she came home. Where he found her didn't matter as much as what he did next. Beat her to death. Then put her in her bed. Turned off his alarm and waited until she was completely cold before he called the police the next morning and made up an elaborate story about driving all around town and finding her battered body in a field.

I know it's true as clearly as I know my name isn't Jennifer Harris. I don't belong here. This isn't my home. There's a life and a family and a future beyond these cement walls, and somehow I'm going to get myself out of this prison. Henry won't let me leave without a fight, but if it comes down to his life or mine, I'm going to win my freedom no matter how much it costs.

EIGHTEEN

JENNIFER STARED at her father in his ugly, beat-up Chevy. She knew she should be afraid, but it took her a half second longer than it should have to wipe that stupid grin off her face, to forget her elation over the absolutely perfect night with Darren. It wasn't until she heard her father's voice that she understood how much trouble she was in.

"I've been looking all over for you." Dad sounded eerily calm. She would have felt far more comfortable if he'd been yelling at her.

"Get in the truck," he growled.

Jennifer hesitated a moment too long. In an instant, her father reached his hand out the window and yanked her by the arm. She hit her head on the side of the door, the dull metallic thump giving way to a high-pitched ringing in her ears.

"Did you go deaf all of a sudden?" Dad growled, his fingernails digging into her flesh. "Get in the truck."

Jennifer heard a noise from the front porch. She glanced over to see Shawna and Kylee standing in front of the house gaping at her.

She scurried over to the passenger side, her head swirling with pain and dizziness.

Her father let out his breath, and Jennifer saw his worried expression, his aged face. "Dad, I'm really …"

"I don't want to hear a word out of you," he snapped. "Not a word, do you understand me? For years, I've done my best to feed you, to clothe you, to keep you safe. Well, how am I supposed to do that when you're sneaking out at all hours of the night, huh? No, I really want you to tell me. How am I supposed to keep you safe?"

Jennifer bit her lower lip, uncertain if her dad wanted an actual answer or not. The corner of her mouth where Darren had given her that kiss still burned hot. For a second, she worried her dad would look over at her and know everything. Everything she and Darren talked about. Everything they did.

She thought about Darren's hand holding hers. About how earnestly he'd looked at her. Nobody had treated her as kindly and lovingly as Darren had tonight. Her father certainly had never been so warm and attentive.

If Mom were still alive, she'd understand. Jennifer could tell her about Darren, ask her questions. Mom would know what you're supposed to say to a boy when you're done with a slow dance. She'd know if you could call a peck that wasn't even quite on the lips a real kiss or just practice.

Jennifer crossed her arms. It wasn't fair. If anybody should have died, it should have been Dad. The euphoria she felt just a few minutes earlier, the confusion and giddy embarrassment that bubbled to the surface when she thought about Darren, the grief that came crashing over her unexpectedly when she remembered Mom … it was impossible to give a name to each and every emotion swirling around chaotically in her soul.

Dad was gripping the steering wheel and muttered something under his breath.

"What did you just say?" Jennifer snapped, her anger now rising to the surface of every other conflicting emotion.

"I said if your mother could see you now, she'd be rolling around in her grave."

Jennifer's fists started flying. "How dare you!" she shouted, punching, scratching, pummeling. "I hate you. Hate you, hate you, HATE you."

Dad jerked the Chevy to a standstill at the bus stop near the school. He turned to her, the tired expression on his face replaced with a look of disgust and rage.

"Get out," he snarled, putting the truck into park.

Jennifer stared for a second, trying to catch her breath, trying to replay what had just happened. Had she really punched her own father? He knew she didn't mean it, right? She didn't really hate him.

"Dad, I'm sorry …"

"Don't give me that." His face was contorted in anger, but his tone was bone-chillingly controlled. "Get out of the truck."

Jennifer hesitated. "I really didn't mean …"

Dad reached across her and flung open the passenger side door. "Get out of the truck," he repeated with a curse.

Jennifer was crying now, not tears of anger but of fear. She raised her eyes to her father, who glowered at her unblinkingly. "What are you going to do to me?" she asked.

Dad adjusted his belt. "I'm going to teach you some manners, young lady, and you better pray you catch on because one wrong move, and I swear I'll make you regret it for the rest of your life."

NINETEEN

I'm shaking by the time we get off the plane. Shaking to the point where my husband has to support me while I walk.

"Are you going to be all right?" one of the gate attendants asks.

"She's not feeling well," Russel answers for me. "I think we need to get her home."

The worker tells Russel something about our bags, the kids are squirrely around me, Andrew's demanding to know what's happening and poor little Annie is confused and thinks we've already landed in Michigan.

"Where are Grandma and Grandpa?" she asks.

I can't focus on any of this. Can't pay

attention to the conversations, the noise. I think about that man in the Hawaiian shirt, about how much he reminded me of Henry. I think about the day I escaped, the same day I discovered what happened to his daughter. I think about Russel, about all the things I should have told him before we got married. I was stupid to think that faith and love alone could erase the memories from my past.

Just like I was stupid to think that I could replace the picture-perfect wife he lost.

We're both broken, Russel and I, but in such different ways. The shattered pieces of our lives in theory might fit together to make something beautiful, but right now we're destroying each other with our lies, our trauma, our grief.

I didn't mean to say it. I should have known better after two years in Henry's basement. But he was so pathetic, sitting there crying, blubbering.

"You're lying," I tell him. I haven't spoken back to him like this since my first few weeks as his prisoner, posing as his daughter, wearing her clothes. I've lost weight, haven't seen the sun in two years.

My muscles are weak, but the hatred I feel for him at this exact minute makes me strong and empowered.

This sniveling old man is nothing to be afraid of. He can't hurt me. Can't touch me. Because I know his secret. I've figured it out. When I look back, I'm pretty sure I've always known but haven't wanted to accept the truth until now. At this precise moment.

Everything Henry and I have gone through together has led to here. Like destiny.

"I know what you did to her," I say, my voice calm and even.

His eyes grow wide. He probably forgot I was still a human with the capacity to speak my own mind.

"You got mad at her for sneaking out. You got mad because she hated you, because she knew you were nothing but a pathetic old man, and you killed her. You knew she was growing up. She liked going to parties now. She was interested in boys. You couldn't keep her home, no matter how hard you tried. And you were terrified of losing her. Terrified that she'd wake up one day and realize what a coward you truly are. You saw it happening, saw the end coming. So you killed her. Because you're sick and twisted and pathetic. You killed her, and you managed to keep enough evidence away from the police that they couldn't actually arrest you or anything. You got away with it, but the guilt's been eating you up inside for years. That's why you've made me pretend to be her. Why you've made me say I forgive you. Well, you know something? I don't forgive you. I hate you. I think you're weak. Pathetic. I can't stand another minute in this house with you. And guess what else. I'm not your daughter. I'm not Jennifer. But if she were here, she wouldn't forgive you either. And she'd be saying the exact same things I am. You're weak. You're nothing. You're a terrible father. And you're totally crazy. You killed her. Killed your own flesh and blood and now the guilt's making you even more miserable and pathetic than ever."

Once the words start pouring out of my mouth, I'm certain that nothing can stop them.

"You say you love her, that you're sorry for what you did to her, but you know what? I don't believe you. I know you meant to kill her. I know what a horrible person you are. You're sick in the brain. She wanted to get away from you. You know that, don't you? And the only way to keep her from despising you was to kill her before she learned how wretched you really are, what a miserable old man …"

And then I stop because Henry's face isn't just contorted in anguish. There's something else there.

"Stop," he gasps. "Help."

I want to keep yelling, telling him that I've finally discovered his secret. I finally know what kind of contemptible human being he truly is, but I can't.

Henry's face is frozen as if carved in stone. He clutches at the collar of his shirt. "Stop," he wheezes. Sweat's dripping down his temples.

My heart quits beating at the sound of his voice. I see his chest make a choppy motion. I don't know what this is. I don't know what's happening.

I jump off the couch and grab a flashlight to see better in the dark. Henry's lips are turning blue, and I realize I'm killing him. Literally killing him.

I reach out for his hand. "What do you need me to do?" I ask. "How can I help?"

I didn't mean to hurt him. Didn't mean to cause him actual physical harm. I just needed to get some things off my chest ...

His chest ...

I place my hand over his heart. Feel how erratically its racing. "What should I do?" I ask.

Henry's face is ashen gray. "Help me," he croaks once more.

I race up the stairs. I try to race up the stairs, is what I should say, but my legs are weak. By the time I'm at the top, I realize I'm about to step into a world I haven't seen in years. I look back down. Is Henry going to stop me? Is he going to yell at me to get back down?

He's bent over himself. I can hear the labored breathing from here. Does he even know I'm at the top of the staircase?

I throw open the door, steel myself for whatever terrors await me on the other side. Monsters. Guard dogs. Soldiers ordered to shoot me on sight. Instead, nothing but blinding daylight streaming in from the windows. I can't see anything. Pain pierces to the back of my skull. I have to help Henry.

I stumble into a messy room, a den or a living room of sorts with trash and molding food strewn everywhere. Is there a phone I can use?

I trip over a takeout box. My hands dart in front of me to break my fall. I scrape my forearm on something. I don't care. Henry is downstairs dying, and it's all my fault. I shouldn't have let my anger take hold of me that way. I should have been more compassionate …

Why doesn't this man have a stupid phone?

I'm looking everywhere. To my left is a front door with three separate dead bolts protecting me from the outside world. I could run outside, yell for help. I glance out a grimy window. All I see is a looming fence surrounding the house, but beyond that must be something.

Can I get help for Henry fast enough?

I've overturned a small table. A shoebox full of photographs has spilled onto the floor at my feet. I pick up one of the pictures. It's of me. There are dozens of them, all close up, photographs of me when I'm sleeping. My skin is pale. I almost look like I'm dead.

My hands are trembling. I don't have time to stop and stare, but I do. Because there's something wrong about the pictures. Something I didn't notice at first.

I don't own a shirt like that. And the sleeping head I'm staring at is resting on a pillow. A real pillow with a real pillowcase, not the hard couch cushion Henry's given me.

Even more surprising, the sleeping girl in the photograph is in a real bed.

And then I realize I'm not looking at pictures of myself at all. It's Henry's dead daughter. I drop the images, my heart speeding wildly. I tell myself I'm running outside to get help. It's the only way I can justify leaving Henry here like this. I hate him. Despise him. Fear him. But the thought of him down there all alone, feeling so remorseful … I can't make myself leave unless I lie. I tell myself I'll run and get him help. I tell myself I'll race down the road, find the nearest house or wave down the nearest car and call 911 to get them to send Henry an ambulance. It's the only thing that allows me to unlock the deadbolts. They're heavier than I expected, as if they've rusted in place.

Hurry, I tell myself, *Henry could die any second.*

Except that's not why I'm hurrying. Not really. I know that once I leave this house, I'm going home, and nothing's going to stop me.

The last bolt finally slides out of place.

The sun hits my skin for the first time since my capture. I don't have time to pause and wonder. My only thought is to get away. Do I go right or left? I don't know. All I know is that I need to put one foot in front of the other. I force myself to be strong, to resist the urge to turn back.

I can't do it. Can't leave him here like this. I think I hear him call my name. "Jennifer." Then I think about the pictures I saw. I think about Henry's dead daughter, about how he's kept me prisoner in his basement. I remember the vaguest notion of a mother and father who loved me once upon a time, and I realize I want to see them again.

I desperately want to see them again.

I know they're out there. And I know I don't belong trapped in a basement for the rest of my life.

I have no idea how long I've been walking. It feels like a lifetime. The houses are set back in the woods. All I see are driveways. One road turns to another. I can't keep the directions straight. I might be walking in circles for all I can tell. I think it must have been an hour, maybe more. Maybe whole days have passed since I ran away from Henry, since I abandoned him alone in that basement to die.

The shadows are long, the evening chilly when I spot a woman walking her dog. My eyes want to spill over with tears. How long has it been since I've seen another human being? Seen an animal of any kind?

My legs threaten to collapse beneath me the moment she comes into view. I wave my arms. She raises her hand but then stops.

"Help," I call out, certain now that my legs can't carry me another step.

She jogs toward me. I don't know if it's my stress or my fear or my physical weakness, but I'm only half conscious when her dog comes up, sniffs me once curiously, then licks my face with a warm tongue.

His kiss makes me start to sob.

The woman kneels down. I can't understand the questions she's asking me, but I hear the worry in her voice.

"I need help," I tell her.

"What's your name?" she asks.

I nearly answer "Jennifer" before I remember. That's not me anymore. It never was me. "My name is Anastasia," I answer. "Anastasia Reynolds. I want to go home."

TWENTY

"Anastasia," my husband snaps.

I gasp in a desperate breath of air. "Russel?" My voice is hoarse. Like I've just been strangled and my windpipe has been bruised.

"Anastasia." He repeats my name. It sounds strange coming from him for some reason. "Are you all right?"

The children are looking at me with fearful expressions, even the older ones. I glance around, half expecting to find myself facing a very alive Henry or locked in his basement again.

But that's not what I see. I'm in the airport. My husband and children — my family — are here staring at me worriedly. Two others, an official-looking man and woman, are standing far too close, asking me questions, feeling my wrists, talking to each other in hushed tones.

"I'm all right," I tell them. I don't know if they're EMTs or airport workers or what, but I can't breathe when they're crowding me like this. "I'm all right," I repeat. I'm not sure who I'm most trying to convince, but I do know that none of them believe me.

It's okay. I don't even believe myself.

"We should get you to a doctor or something," Russel says. "Is there someone who can give her a checkup?" he asks.

I don't hear the woman's response. I'm too busy reminding myself that I'm here. I'm alive. I'm safe.

More strangers approach. An old lady asks if Russel needs help watching the kids. My head is spinning, my whole body clammy.

"I think she's coming down with something," Russel tells the concerned onlookers.

I convince my husband in no uncertain terms that I will not be pushed through the airport in a wheelchair. He gives the gate attendants what must be his dozenth apology, then he gathers the children from where they've been seated, watching me fall apart.

"What's wrong with her?" Andrew asks.

"Mom's just a little tired," he says, "that's all." Russel looks over at me, his eyes full of concern. Of fear. Of love.

I shouldn't have kept this from him for so long. I had no reason not to tell him before. Do I have the courage now to make things right? Or will that only make everything so much worse?

Why didn't you tell me sooner? I'm certain that's the question he'll ask when he learns the truth. And then, even once I come clean, how will he believe anything else I tell him from now on? He wouldn't trust me. I wouldn't trust me if I were in his shoes.

The Bible says to tell the truth, right? But it also says that we need to work hard to make our marriages last. So what am I supposed to do?

We're early enough into the relationship. There may be cause for an annulment. I've looked it up. We were both in our right minds getting married. Neither of us were coerced or anything like that. But the state will annul a marriage in the case of fraud. Does lying about my past count as fraud? What about the fact that I never told Russel about my infertility? I was pregnant when I ran away from Henry's. Neither of us knew it at the time. I miscarried the week after my rescue. My mother insists it was the shock. My father believed it was a merciful act of God. Either way, the resulting hemorrhaging and complications have left me unable to bear children.

I was too riddled with guilt over having left Henry to die that I hardly thought about the other life I lost. Never mourned the inability to ever conceive again.

I tried telling the policemen where Henry's house was, but I'd been walking for so long before I found help. I couldn't retrace my steps, no matter how hard I tried.

I told them he was sick. I told them he was old, he was weak, he was having a heart attack or something. I told them I shouldn't have left him all alone. They told me I'd done the right thing, the brave thing, the only thing I could have done to get myself out of a terrible situation.

I still have nightmares that Henry's dying

in that basement, begging me for help, pleading with me to save his life.

A week and a half later, the police called my parents to let them know. A man had been discovered dead in his home. The basement was just as I described.

Henry was gone. My mother was ecstatic. My father furious that my captor would never stand trial.

"God himself'll judge that monster," he'd say. "It's the most we can hope for now."

I did what I could to try to adjust to life back home. Mom and Dad had left my room exactly as it had been, but the mattress was too lumpy, the pillow too soft. I woke up every night burning up from the heat. All that winter my parents kept the thermostat set at 62.

I remember that season after my escape like I remember watching documentaries in history class. I study them clinically, wonder if the final bullet that killed my parents' marriage was the stress of my abduction or the turmoil they experienced when they realized the carefree child they lost was gone forever, dead and buried in Henry's basement.

I didn't cry, didn't lash out. Mom was worried for me, begged me to open up and tell her what was wrong. I didn't want to talk.

I just wanted to forget.

TWENTY-ONE

"Feeling better now?" my husband asks me.

I try in vain to offer him a smile. "Yeah. I think you're right. I must be coming down with something."

I've lost track of how long we've been here. At least an hour, maybe more. After I calmed down, it took three different agents to help us locate our bags. Now we're waiting near some back office for the airport workers to grab our luggage and wheel it out to us. I forget how many times I've apologized to Russel for ruining his vacation.

"You and the kids should go on without me," I insist, but of course he won't leave me.

He's already called his parents. I have no idea what he told them, nor do I want to. I just want to go home. Get out of here. I feel like every pair of eyes is staring at me.

What was it about that man on the airplane that got me so freaked out? The Hawaiian shirt? The way the girl he was with looked so uncomfortable?

I should tell someone. Maybe.

But tell them what?

Hey, there was this weirdo on the plane traveling with a teen girl and … I don't know. I just didn't like the way he looked?

It's ridiculous. Just like it's ridiculous for me to even think about telling Russel about why I started to panic. I know my husband. If he knew about Henry, he'd just pity me and worry about me, and I'd feel even more suffocated under his loving care. That's exactly what happened after I escaped Henry's basement and tried to live back home.

I try to remember how long it's been since I called my mom, but I can't. Her birthday was three months ago, but I know I missed it.

"Mommy?" Annie grabs my hand. "I need to go potty."

I'm thankful for something to do. Something that only I can do. I remind myself that I'm an adult. I'm the responsible one. I'm probably just coming down with the flu or something like that. Russel already asked me after we got off the plane if I thought I was pregnant. I wish my outburst could be chalked up to some kind of hormonal imbalance.

I should be so lucky.

I tell Russel I'm taking Annie to the bathroom, and while I wait outside her stall, I have a little time to think. Take a few deep breaths, try to compose myself. I'm not in any danger. Nobody is trying to capture me or force me to wear someone else's clothes and pretend to be their murdered daughter.

I'm safe. I'm here with my family. I'm a grown woman, a wife, a survivor.

Nothing can hurt me here.

Annie starts humming a song to herself, one clue out of many that she's going to take her sweet and precious time. The bathroom isn't crowded, and I pace the length of the stalls. Anything to get my mind off that airplane, that teen girl I saw. The one with scared, haunted eyes.

Suddenly I'm dizzy. I know my mind's

about to send me right back to Henry's basement. I've got to get control of myself.

My breath comes in choppy spurts. "I'm going to be in the stall right next to you," I tell Annie, and I shut the door behind me. Something about the enclosed space makes me feel more at ease. Less exposed.

There's a small poster taped above the toilet paper.

It is estimated that at least twenty thousand minors are trafficked in the United States every year.

My stomach flips once. Twice. I press my palm against my abdomen to try to stop the sloshing.

Questions you can ask yourself if you see something suspicious: Does the potential victim in question act confused, submissive, or afraid?

"I can't reach the toilet paper," Annie calls to me. I manage to find the voice to tell her I need a minute.

Do they avoid eye contact?

The image of that girl on the plane flashes again in my mind. I tell myself I'm overreacting. I'm projecting my own experience and trauma onto a situation that's none of my business.

Is the potential victim wearing appropriate attire?

It's this question that literally sucks the breath out of my lungs.

"Mommy!" Annie whines.

"Just a minute." I need to think. Was that what finally gave it away? A T-shirt and shorts? There was no crime in dressing inappropriately for the season.

I squeeze my eyes shut, compose my breathing as best as I can, then unlock the door. I help Annie finish and wash up, and I hold her hand as we make our way back to her father. Russel's standing with our luggage. I can't tell if he looks tired or annoyed or concerned. I'm dizzy. My mind can hardly focus on anything.

"There's a problem," I tell him as soon as I'm at his side. "I need to talk to someone from security."

TWENTY-TWO

JENNIFER STARED AT HER FATHER. Was he seriously kicking her out of the truck this late at night?

"Get out," he growled again and made a lunge toward her.

She jumped onto the curb, afraid her father would come after her, afraid he'd slap her right then and there for sneaking out, for talking back, for getting angry and hitting him.

What she didn't expect was for him to slam the Chevy door and drive off.

She stood there on the sidewalk in front of the school, shivering in the cold, waiting for the red glow of his taillights.

Dad sped through a stop sign and disappeared from view.

Jennifer hugged herself to ward off the cold and waited. Ten minutes. Fifteen minutes. Had he already gone home?

When she was finally convinced that he wasn't returning for her, she felt into her pockets for change. She didn't have any coins left, and even if she did, she didn't know who she should call. Shawna? Kylee?

She had Darren's number memorized. Even though she'd never called him before, she'd spent hours staring at his last name in the phone book, wondering if one day she'd ever have the courage to give him a ring.

It couldn't be tonight, though. What she had to ask herself was whose parents would be the most likely to be awake past midnight. That and who would be least likely to get upset if Jennifer woke them up.

She could walk home, but it was totally dark out. Dark and freezing. She wished Darren were here with her. She couldn't believe that such a short time ago she was sitting next to him on Kylee's couch, their legs touching. He'd kissed her, right? What if he'd only been trying to give her a hug and his lips accidentally touched hers? Did that still count?

What if he already regretted spending time with her?

What if he and Lisa were together right now?

She couldn't think like this. It was late, but Kylee must still be awake. Jennifer could call her or just walk over to her place. She could walk to Kylee's and spend the night there. Give her dad time to sleep it off. In the morning, he wouldn't be so upset.

She still couldn't believe he'd driven off like that. For a split second, Jennifer was sickened by a terrifying thought. What if her dad had gotten into a car accident? What if he'd only been planning to scare her, to teach her a lesson, and he had a heart attack behind the wheel or something? Just last week, the doctor had told him he needed to exercise more and lose weight. The tiny aspirin pill he took once a day wasn't enough to keep his heart healthy as he got older.

Was it possible something had happened to her dad? She had to find out.

She took a step off the curb then saw headlights coming down from the school parking lot. Good. Her dad really had just meant to scare her. He probably drove around the neighborhood until he figured she was adequately spooked, then drove through the football field entrance and was coming back now to pick her up.

He'd apologize when she got into the truck, but she wasn't going to let him get off so easily. What had he been thinking?

The car slowed down, but it wasn't until it was just a few feet away from the curb when Jennifer realized it wasn't her father after all.

"Jennifer Harris? Is that you? What in the world are you doing out here? Get in the car."

He leaned over to open the passenger door. Jennifer hadn't realized until now how much she'd been shivering.

She gave him a little smile, hoping he wouldn't ask too many questions. What would she tell him to explain how she ended up out here in the cold?

He locked the doors as she was buckling up. "You must be freezing." His voice was full of worry. He sounded so concerned for her safety, Jennifer thought she might start crying.

"Let me turn up the heat," he said, and

soon the hot air was blowing on her at full blast.

"First question for you," he said when Jennifer's teeth finally stopped chattering. "Are you safe?"

She nodded.

"Are you hurt?"

"No."

He let out a relieved sigh. "That's all I wanted to know. Now, tell me where you need to go. Let's get you out of this cold."

TWENTY-THREE

I EXPECT Russel to ask me more questions, to demand to know everything that's going on. Maybe he's resigned to the fact that his new wife is a nutcase. Maybe he is just trying to do whatever he can do to appease me.

"Are you sure this girl was in trouble?" is all he asks.

I shake my head. "I can't say. It's just, the guy she was with gave me a really bad feeling …"

I don't know how else to respond. I'm still surprised that Russel hasn't told me I'm overreacting, that after the scene I've already made on the plane there's no need to conjure up an encore performance here.

Let's just take our bags and go home. That's

what I want him to say. Instead, he stops someone wearing an airlines nametag. "Excuse me, is there someone from security I can speak to?"

For the next fifteen minutes, my face burns hot as I sit behind a desk answering a stranger's questions.

"Did you have any interaction with the passenger in question?" "Did the girl you noticed say anything to you or try to signal you in any way?" "Did you overhear any conversation between this girl and the man she was traveling with?"

Now that I'm getting interrogated about two individuals I've never met in my life, I realize what a mistake I made insisting on speaking to security. I've lost track of how many times I've told this officer that I was just overreacting on the plane. It's nothing. I'm sorry for wasting his time.

Russel and the kids are waiting for me outside the cramped office. I can only imagine what's running through my husband's brain right now. Is he wondering what his parents think of me? Is he ashamed of my outburst on the plane? Maybe he's wondering how to tell his kids that their new stepmom is certifiably insane.

I'm shaking by the time we're done. The officer did a good job listening to my concerns, asked all the right questions. The problem is I don't have any actual evidence. Nothing tangible to go on but the fact that a girl was wearing shorts and a T-shirt in the winter. But what does that prove? Maybe her next stop after Detroit was Hawaii for all I know.

My face is burning when I join Russel and the children.

"Everything okay?" he asks me.

I smile. "Yeah, I think …" I don't know what to tell him. "I'm sorry for ruining the trip." It's the best I can do.

His voice is gentle. "Don't worry about that. I talked to a gate agent while you were having your meeting. They got us on another flight. We leave in three hours."

My stomach sinks. It was stupid for me not to have expected this. Russel's glowing and raving on and on about what a huge blessing it is they were able to squeeze six of us on a flight together, and all I can think is I wish the attendant told him there was room for Russel and the kids but not for me.

I need time. Time to catch my breath. To remind myself that just because a girl's wearing shorts doesn't mean her life's in danger. That just because I was captured and locked away for two years it doesn't mean every other teenager with sad, haunted eyes is going through the same horror. The trauma I went through.

I had only been home for three months after escaping Henry's basement when a policeman knocked on our door. I hated him and that stupid Styrofoam cup of coffee he always carried around with him.

"We've had a new development," he said, stepping into our home without waiting to be invited. "Call your mom in. She'll want to hear this."

And then the officer proceeded to tell me the truth that's going to haunt me until the day I die.

Henry hadn't killed his daughter.

Concerning the murder of Jennifer Harris, Henry was completely innocent.

TWENTY-FOUR

Jennifer hadn't seen Mr. Green in a while. It had been a full two years since she was a student in his science class. He seemed different now. But maybe that was because she was looking at him through the tears she was desperately trying to blink away.

"So," Mr. Green said as he put his car into gear. "I'm not going to ask what you were doing, but if you wanted someone to talk to about it, I'm all ears." He had a sign for some old band dangling from his rearview mirror. Back in middle school, Jennifer and her friends had spent hours speculating on the rumors that Mr. Green did drugs every night, that he'd been in a rock band in college, that he kept a shrine to the

Grateful Dead in his attic. When Kylee's older brother told the girls that Mr. Green was suspected to have dated one of his former students once she came home from college, the rumor mill seemed to have a limitless supply of fodder.

How much of it was true? Jennifer wondered. Mr. Green was strange. There was no denying that, but at least his car heater worked.

"Where am I taking you to, m'lady?" he asked, his voice happy and good-natured.

Jennifer's jaw hurt from clenching it while she stood outside in the cold. She tried to will her body to relax a degree but wasn't sure she was that successful. She sniffed loudly and hoped Mr. Green didn't think she was crying.

"I live over on Belview."

"Belview?" he repeated. "I know right where that is," Mr. Green answered enthusiastically. "It would be my great honor and privilege to take you wherever you need to go."

Jennifer glanced at him out of the corner of her eye. Tried to determine which if any of the rumors about her former teacher were true.

"How are you liking high school?" Mr. Green asked. "You're a sophomore now?"

"Freshman," she answered.

"Really? I could have sworn you were older." Mr. Green glanced over at her. "Are you doing all right? Or does the fact that I found you on the corner alone with your makeup all smeared answer that question for me?" He waited for an answer.

Jennifer stayed silent.

Finally, Mr. Green let out a sigh. "Well, I know it's not any of my business," he finally announced, "but I do tend to worry about my students. Teacher's curse, I'm afraid. I worry about each and every one of you."

"Mm-hmm." Jennifer squirmed in her seat. Something was making her uncomfortable. Maybe she shouldn't have gotten in the car with Mr. Green after all. Maybe she should have just asked him for some change so she could call her dad, beg him to come pick her up.

It wasn't until then that she realized they were driving the wrong way. She tried to remember. She'd told him Belview, right?

"I think my home's the other way." She kept her voice low, didn't want him to think she was ungrateful for his help.

"Oh." Mr. Green gave the steering wheel a small slap and let out a chuckle. "I'm sorry, I must have been driving on auto-pilot. I'm taking you straight to my house."

Jennifer glanced at the time on his dashboard. Wondered why she hadn't thought to ask what Mr. Green was doing driving around town this late in the first place.

"Hey, I've got to pick something up at the middle school. You okay if we take a quick detour?"

Jennifer couldn't guess what he had to do at the school this late, but Mr. Green was already going way out of his way to get her home. She couldn't be rude. "No problem." She tried to make her voice sound at ease. Tried to mask the growing discomfort she felt. Tried to tell herself that in a few more minutes, she'd be back home in her warm bed and the stress of the night would be nothing but a distant memory.

TWENTY-FIVE

GIVEN the status of what remains in my backpack, I grossly underestimated how many snacks I'd need to pack to keep four children and two adults from growing hungry. Our newly booked flight doesn't start boarding for another hour, but I know better than to ask Russel to spend money on airport food.

I'm feeling much better now. Finally got over whatever shock I had. In fact, I'm actually glad Russel was able to get our family on this other plane. I would hate to think that I've ruined this vacation for everyone. Yes, I'm still anxious about meeting the in-laws. Still terrified that every single thing I do, every word I say will be compared to Sarah. Russel's parents loved his first wife like a daughter. He hasn't told me this, but his sister has. Their whole family saw her as one of their own.

They're all still mourning her death.

Which is exactly why I was dreading this trip.

But there's nothing like a massive panic attack on a crowded airplane to put things into perspective. I'm a survivor. I can't even guess how many times I've reminded myself of that fact since I finished talking with airport security. The man was attentive enough, but he realized as soon as we started talking that there was nothing to go on. I have no idea why I got so upset in the first place. What did I expect him to do? Order the captain to turn the plane around so they could arrest a man simply because his teenage daughter wore shorts and a surly expression?

As humiliated as I am by the experience, I think in the end it's all for the best. I've forgotten how much energy it takes me to keep everything that happened with Henry hidden, secret, and forgotten. My trauma is a trapped animal, expending all its effort trying to get out of its cage. It's a full-time job keeping my demons in check.

I've promised myself I'll tell Russel everything. But not right now. Not here in the airport, not until we're home after this vacation. But he deserves to know. I won't tell him in a way that makes him feel sorry for me or worried about my mental health. I'll just bring it up casually. *Hey, there's something I didn't feel totally comfortable telling you earlier, but now that we're married, I think it's important for you to know.*

That's the kind of conversation two rational adults can have, right?

Picturing this future encounter holds my guilt at bay, the guilt I feel for not exposing my secrets earlier. Eventually I'll tell Russel everything. When the time is right. Might be next month, might be in a year … The longer I wait, the more awkward it'll be, but then again, by that point our marriage will be stronger. More resilient.

Who am I kidding?

This is a secret I might as well carry with me to my grave.

"We should have packed more sandwiches," Russel announces factually. I love how he uses the pronoun *we*, as if he had any part in packing for this trip for six. But who am I to complain? It's my fault we're here and not on our way to his parents' already. If I hadn't overreacted like I did, we'd be landing in Detroit any minute.

"Look, Daddy," Andrew says, pointing at a TV screen. "It's an airplane."

Russel glances up. I'm still rummaging through my carry-on, looking for more food to pass around, when I hear my husband suck in his breath.

My eyes follow his gaze. The ticker at the bottom of the screen reads *Flight hijacked. Missing Detroit teen identified as one of the passengers.* A school photo accompanies the text. Blood drains from my brain. I'm glad I'm sitting because the room has tilted onto its axis.

Russel grabs my hand. "Is that …?" He doesn't complete his sentence. He doesn't have the chance.

Three men and one woman in very professional-looking suits walk directly up to me, brandishing official badges. "Are you Anastasia Strickland? You talked earlier with one of our security officers?"

I give a faint nod and try to tell them yes. I can't even hear my own voice, but that doesn't seem to matter to these agents.

"Come with us, please. We have some questions for you."

TWENTY-SIX

Russel refuses to let me go anywhere without him. It's sweet, actually. A little protective.

It takes a few minutes, but the airlines agents call in someone to keep an eye on the kids in the adjoining room and take my husband and me to another small office. Through the cracks in the door, I hear Andrew whining about how hungry he is.

"Mrs. Strickland, are you aware of what's occurring aboard Flight 219?"

"I saw something on the news," I answer, uncertain if this is what I'm supposed to say or not. "I don't really understand …"

"Flight 219 has been hijacked," the man

interrupts. "And as part of the attack, the perpetrators have kidnapped the daughter of Detroit's school district superintendent."

I don't understand what a school district has to do with hijacked planes or acts of terrorism. A small portion of my brain worries that I've misheard everything this man is telling me.

I'm thankful when Russel leans forward in his seat and takes the lead. "That's the same girl my wife mentioned. The one she talked to the security officer about." I don't know how to describe what I hear in his voice. Is he angry they didn't listen to me in the first place? Scared to think that his entire family was supposed to be aboard that plane? The only name I can give to his tone is intense.

The officer nods his head. "Yes. We took your wife's concerns very seriously when she brought them to our attention, and in the end, it seems she was right to sound the alarm."

"What's happening to those people right now?" my husband asks.

"I assure you we have every available law enforcement agency and officer involved to

ensure they don't harm anyone else in their
..."

"I mean the passengers," Russel interrupts. "What's happening to them? Are they
all right?"

"News is just coming in," the agent answers. "I'm afraid that's all I can tell you
right now."

I'm trembling. I'm afraid I'm going to
throw up my peanut butter and jelly sand-
wich and granola bar. So I wasn't wrong. I
wasn't crazy. I wasn't making things up.

Which means that girl really was stolen
from her parents. That she really was as terrified as she appeared.

I should have done more. Asked her for
her name, found a way to talk to her alone.
What was I thinking? I just left her there, left
her alone her with her abductor ... And now
the plane's been hijacked.

She must be so scared.

I want to know everything about her.
Her age. Her favorite color. What kind of
music she listens to. The name of her crush.
I want to know where she sleeps at night, in
a bed safe and warm or in a freezing cold
basement, her hands cuffed behind her
back.

And the man with her, who is he? Has he just abducted her, or has she been trapped with him for weeks? Months? Has she gotten to the point where she's forgotten her age? Where she's certain at least one birthday has passed but all she can do is wonder what her parents did to commemorate the day …

An agent who's been silently standing in the corner speaks up. His partner turns around, and they have a small huddle in hushed tones, using words and phrases that cascade over me.

I squeeze my eyes shut. Russel puts his arm around me. Draws me close.

"I'm so glad you got us off that plane," he whispers. "That must have been God guiding you."

There's nothing but awe in Russel's voice, except I can't share his sense of grateful relief. Because that girl is still on that plane with her captor. And the other passengers … I can't even imagine what's happening to them.

"… demanding to speak to the superintendent," one of the agents is saying, and they continue talking about some elementary playground. I can't believe that an abduction and hijacking all revolve around school politics, but what do I know? After I escaped Henry's basement, I never even returned to school. I got my degree from a correspondence program, which meant my mother didn't need to let me out of her sight. Which meant I never had to leave the house.

If you were to ask Mom the details, I was in shock when I first returned home. Then came the miscarriage. The hemorrhaging. The surgery. A few months later, once my body healed and I realized I didn't have to simply exist in survival mode anymore, I broke down and fell into an unbreakable depression.

The real depression was because I had discovered the truth. I'm the reason Henry died. I killed him. His heart gave out when I accused him of murdering his daughter. I was so sure of it at the time. But I'd been wrong. Dead wrong. The cop who came to our house that day told me that they reopened Jennifer's case, that they found a DNA match.

Henry hadn't killed Jennifer after all.

Which meant I broke Henry's heart when I accused him. I'm the one who killed him.

Mom couldn't understand. "Whether or not he murdered his daughter, he was a monster. He kept you trapped in a basement for two full years." She stated the words so factually, as if she expected them to break through my despair and get me to see reason.

Henry hadn't killed Jennifer. How many times had he begged me to tell him I believed him? That I knew he'd never lift a hand to hurt me?

And then one day I snapped. I yelled those terrible things at him, accused him of those monstrous acts.

I killed him with my words.

I'm a survivor. Some would say I did what I had to do. I escaped with my life, didn't I? Do you know how rare it is to survive two years of captivity?

Going strictly by the numbers, I should have been dead within the first 48 hours.

I'm a statistical anomaly.

I survived. I got myself out of there.

Now I'm free.

Free from Henry's basement. Free from his handcuffs. Free from his delusions. Free from his oppressive grief.

Free from everything. Everything except the overwhelming guilt I felt that I accused a weak, sad man of a crime he didn't commit, then I ran away when he needed my help the most and left him to die, terrified and alone.

TWENTY-SEVEN

"Are you crying?" Russel asks me.

His voice is so gentle. So pained to think I might be in any sort of turmoil or anguish.

"I don't want to answer any more questions." I choke on the words. I didn't expect to break so easily.

The agents turn and look at me.

"We need to go," Russel tells them. "My wife is unwell."

He doesn't wait for their permission but stands me up, holding onto my elbow. My legs nearly collapse under me.

"Are you all right?" he asks, worried. "Do you need a doctor? Is there a doctor she can see? I think it's the stress. She isn't well …"

I hear the hint of panic in his voice, and that's when I crack. I let the pieces of my soul that I've tried so desperately to hold together all these years crumble to shards around me.

"She's in shock or something," my husband insists, and still it takes the men in the room several seconds staring at us before one of them says, "I'll see what I can do."

Russel is trying to support my weight, trying to keep me from falling to the ground. I can't stand the feel of his fingers clenching my arm, can't stand the memory of Henry's grip on my body.

"Let me go," I shriek, only half aware that I'm yelling at my own husband and not a man who's been dead for ten years. "I don't want to stay here. I want to leave."

A childlike voice from the doorway carries over the sound of my hyperventilating. "What's wrong with Mommy? Is she all right?"

I don't process the child's words or Russel's answer. Someone's hurrying toward me. Seconds later an oxygen monitor is clasped to my finger, a blood pressure gauge wrapped around my arm.

"Has she had anything to eat or drink lately?" a voice asks my husband.

"Here, someone take my wallet and go get her something from McDonalds," he says, and I want to laugh at the thought of Russel ordering me fast food.

My breath returns to me in short, choppy gulps. I want to pass out. I want to ignore the faces around me, the worried expressions, the shouted questions.

"She's unwell." I've lost track of how many times Russel has repeated himself. *Unwell, unwell, unwell …*

My wife is unwell.

The man has no idea.

No idea whatsoever.

TWENTY-EIGHT

JENNIFER FELT silly for getting herself so worked up. Just because it was dark out, just because there was nobody out on any of the roads this late at night, she didn't have to create all kinds of spooky stories about her teacher. She blamed Shawna and Kylee and all their silly rumors about Mr. Green from all the way back in middle school.

He'd kept the car running while he ran into the school to get whatever it was he'd left. Jennifer was glad the heater was on. First of all, she was still freezing cold. Second of all, it made her certain that whatever Mr. Green was here to do, it wouldn't take long.

For a minute, she wished she'd asked if

she could go inside with him, but she didn't want to make it seem like she was afraid to stay out here alone. She wasn't the same little pre-teen she'd been when she was a student in his science class so long ago. She was older now, far more mature.

Now that her body had started to warm and her mind was no longer fixating on the problem of how to get herself home, she found herself remembering her evening at the party with Darren. She couldn't wait to see him at school on Monday. Maybe she'd even see him sooner than that. Her heart gave a little leap to her throat at the thought, and she immersed herself in playing out the various scenarios. Maybe she'd go to the mall tomorrow with Lisa and Shawna and Kylee, and he'd be there with his older brother, and they'd see each other and smile and break off from their respective groups and go ice skating together.

Maybe Lisa would decide that she didn't want to be outdone by Kylee's party, so she'd throw a party of her own tomorrow night, and Jennifer and Darren would meet up again there.

Maybe it'd be a total fluke where you knew it had to be God making things work out, and she'd run into him while she went to the grocery store with her dad to pick up something for dinner.

For the first time in her recent memory, she felt truly happy. She was so lost in her thoughts she gasped when someone flung open the passenger side door of the car.

She gave a little jump, then let out her breath when she realized who it was. "You scared me," she said with a giggle, a giggle that died on her lips the moment she saw his face. Something wasn't right. Something was terribly wrong.

"Get out of the car," he told her, and that's when she saw the knife in his hand. It was one of those dissecting tools she remembered from that frog lab that made her and Shawna both feel sick.

"Get out," Mr. Green repeated.

Jennifer glanced once more at his scalpel and did what he said.

TWENTY-NINE

It's almost nighttime before we load the car to drive home, our bags in the trunk and our flight plans forgotten. The kids are disappointed their vacation's ruined. Russel's decided not to tell them the specifics of the hijacked airplane. They know there was a problem with one of the airplanes, and that's why we're not going to see Grandma and Grandpa after all.

What they don't know is that the same airplane that crash landed in Detroit was the airplane we were seated on earlier today. That we were hours away from what could have been our deaths.

Russel's mom insisted on talking to me when he called. She tells me I'm a prophetess, that I have the gift of discernment, that God saved our family by giving me divine insight into what was about transpire on that plane.

I didn't have the heart to tell her otherwise.

Russel still thinks my emotional reactions today are all related to the hunch I got that something wasn't right with our flight. News reports have been filing in all evening. Apparently, the Detroit school district ordered an elementary school to be built on toxic wasteland. A few parents were upset enough they got up in arms, literally. Kidnapping the superintendent's daughter to use her as a bargaining chip. Hampering with the electric wiring in the airplane lavatory to cause a fire. I still don't know all the facts. Not sure how many people died.

The truth is I don't want to know any more details than I already do.

The kidnapped girl is safe now. I didn't realize how much tension I'd been holding in my body until I saw the news coverage showing her reunited with her parents. Does she know about me, I wonder? Will the federal agents who are debriefing her right now let her know that some unnamed passenger got off the plane and sounded the alarm?

I'm not sure it really matters. I might have been right about her being a victim, but that didn't stop the plane from getting hijacked.

"Look, Daddy! It's Chuck E. Cheese! Just like the one Grandma and Grandpa take us to!"

I certainly can't imagine Russel being the type of father who'd let his children into a venue like Chuck E. Cheese. It makes me wonder if his parents are more lenient than he is. Or maybe Annie's referring to her mother's parents.

Regardless, I'm shocked when Russel turns on his blinker and pulls into the parking lot. "What are you doing?" I ask.

He shrugs. "The kids are hungry."

Squeals erupt from the back seats. Russel grins at me sheepishly. I wonder if I'm sup-posed to keep our family excursion to Chuck E. Cheese a secret from the congregation. Or maybe I'm reading too much into it.

The children don't seem nearly as out of place as I feel. When they get inside, they hold their arms out expertly so the workers can mark their hands. I don't realize until

Russel follows suit that adults are given the same kind of stamp. Indisputable proof that our family belongs together, I suppose.

Russel pulls out two twenty dollar bills and tells Betsy to get tokens and divide them evenly. "Stay together," he gives as a final ultimatum, and the children race off.

I blink, wondering if my husband's mind is simply reacting to the stress and shock of the day. Never in our entire engagement did I picture our family hanging out in Chuck E. Cheese. I want to ask him what the members of Gospel Kingdom would think, but he looks so happy I don't bring it up.

"Are you hungry?" he asks then shocks me again by ordering two large pepperoni pizzas. We wait for our food at an empty table, and he takes me by the hand.

"I'm so glad you were with us today. I'm so glad God gave you that warning and that you heeded it and got our family off that flight."

I take a deep breath. On the wall behind my husband, robotic rodents dance on stage. The strobing lights are distracting enough I'm surprised we're not all suffering seizures yet.

Russel gives my hand a squeeze. "You

really are amazing, you know that? You probably saved our family's life today."

I'm about to tell him. I'm about to tell him everything, but he isn't giving me the chance.

"That took a lot of courage," he continues. "And I'll admit, I was worried at first. I thought maybe you were having second thoughts about meeting my parents. The last couple days have felt a little ..." He leaves the thought unfinished.

"It's been kind of stressful," I admit.

He nods, as if I've just confirmed what he'd been wanting to say but couldn't. He squeezes my hand again and lets out a chuckle. "For a minute, I thought you wanted off the plane to get away from me."

I smile back at him, but I can't force myself to feel any joy or relief. There's so much he doesn't know.

Betsy comes running up. Andrew's got a scrape on his knee and needs a bandage. Good thing I've got half a dozen in my purse.

I may not be the world's most experienced mother, but I'm a fast learner.

I hand Betsy the Band-Aid, tell her to wash her hands before and after putting it on, and the entire time my husband stares at me as if in shock.

"You're amazing," he says. "You really are. I see you with the kids, I see how much you love them, what a great mom you are, and I realize just how blessed I am. I thank God so much for bringing you into my life."

I want to ask him about Sarah. Want to ask if he thinks I'll ever come close to being the wife or mother she was. I want to ask if he sometimes has doubts too, if he wonders whether or not we should have waited before getting married so quickly.

I want to ask if he has second thoughts.

But I don't.

I'm thinking about that girl from the airplane, wondering what it will be like now that she's been returned to her parents. The good news, if you can call it that, was she was missing for less than 48 hours from the time of her abduction.

She beat the statistical odds.

Lucky her.

"What are you thinking about?" Russel asks.

I picture myself telling him everything. Just opening up my mouth and vomiting out the truth. *I'm thinking about the man who kidnapped me. He held me trapped in his basement for two years and then I caused him to have a heart attack when I accused him of murdering his daughter. Oh, he didn't murder her by the way. She was killed by a schoolteacher who beat her and drugged her and left her on a football field for dead, but the police figured that part out later.*

By then, Henry was already gone. And I'm the one who killed him.

The words are so close to the tip of my tongue I can nearly taste them. "Can I tell you something?" Immediately I'm interrupted by the worker who comes with our food. Our children must have pizza radar. They're swarming the table in seconds, and it seems almost as quick until they're gone again, leaving half-eaten slices and tomato-stained napkins in their wake.

"I should warn you they have monstrous appetites," Russel says with a grin.

This time I manage to laugh, but the sound is hollow and unconvincing.

He holds my hand gingerly in his. I wonder if Sarah took the kids to Chuck E. Cheese like this. If they ate pizza like this. If he held her hand like this.

"You're so beautiful," Russel breathes.

"Have I ever told you how blessed I am to have you in my life?"

He sounds so sincere. I can feel the love he's pouring into my soul at this exact moment. Our relationship might not be the most conventional, but the love we have for each other is real. I'm not sure I ever realized that until this very moment.

I think about Russel on the airplane, how he didn't question or complain when I told him I needed off. How he stayed by my side when the agents were asking me questions, how he did everything in his power to try to comfort me when I was falling apart piece by piece in front of him.

"I'm blessed to you have you in my life too," I assure him then clear my throat.

The setting is far from idyllic. The music is way too loud. The stage rodents are still dancing just a few feet away from us. Any second one of our children will come running up and interrupt our conversation.

But if I wait for the perfect time to get it all out, it will never happen.

There are two things I know right now. That I love Russel more than anything.

And I trust him.

It's time for me to make things right.

"There's something I've been meaning to tell you." I test the words, noting how they taste in my mouth. I admit that I have no idea how our conversation is going to go after this. I don't know if Russel's going to be hurt that I didn't tell him sooner or if he'll jump into fix-it mode like he did at the airport and try to figure out what he could possibly do to take away the pain of my past.

He might be angry. Might yell at me, demand to know why I kept something so huge a secret from him. But I do know his love for me will never change, and that conviction gives me the courage to grab hold of his hand and look him in the eyes. My gaze doesn't waver.

"Something happened to me when I was younger I never told you about," I begin.

He looks startled. Surprised. Perhaps even a little nervous.

But the love and protectiveness I saw earlier is still there, shining even more brightly as flashing lights and deafening music surround us and blast our senses.

I take a deep breath, wondering if he can feel the way my hand shakes.

Russel thinks I have some sort of divine intuition. His mother calls it the gift of discernment. I certainly don't claim to be a prophet, but I suppose there are certain things I just know even though I can't explain why.

What I know right now is that even though what I'm about to tell Russel will surprise him, even though it will be incredibly hard for him to hear, God is going to use this conversation to make our relationship stronger than it's ever been before.

"The reason I reacted like I did at the airport, the reason I could spot that girl and why I was so upset afterward wasn't because I've got some magical gift from the Lord. It's because I was kidnapped as a teenager." The truth pours out from my mouth. There's no more lights, no more noise. Even the children have been infused with the miraculous ability to entertain themselves without coming to interrupt us.

It's just me and Russel. Us and the painful secrets of my past.

I tell him about everything. Henry's basement. The night he died. His daughter's murder that went unsolved for so long.

"I'm sorry," I conclude, and for what feels like a lifetime, my husband remains completely stone-faced and silent.

"Why are you apologizing?" he finally asks.

"For not telling you sooner. I wanted to. I just … I couldn't talk about it. I thought I was over it. I thought I'd moved on. I just …" I take in a choppy breath. "I'm so sorry I lied to you." I nearly choke on the words. "But you deserve to know the truth."

Russel gets out of his seat then. Comes over to my side of the table and kneels down just like he did the night he proposed.

"You're the woman I love," he says. "You're the woman I chose to marry. You're everything to me."

I shake my head and pull my hand free to wipe away my tears. "I'm not who you think I am," I say, choking a little on the words.

He reaches his arms out toward me. Wraps me in a strong, protective hug. "You're everything I've ever needed or wanted," he whispers.

"You're everything to me too," I answer back.

And I realize then that that's the perfect truth.